WINGS OF EARTH: ONE

ECHOES

OF

STARLIGHT

Other works by Eric Michael Craig

Atlas and the Winds
Book One: Stormhaven Rising
Book Two: Prometheus and the Dragon
Box Set: Atlas and the Winds

Shan Takhu Legacy
Book One: Legacy of Pandora
Book Two: Fulcrum of Odysseus
Book Three: Redemption of Sisyphus
Box Set: Shan Takhu Legacy

Wings of Earth
Book One: Echoes of Starlight
Book Two: Dust of the Deep
Book Three: Chains of Dawn
Book Four: Beyond the Edge
Book Five: Stranger Bedfellows
Book Six: Ghost in the Dark
Book Seven: Hope Dies Hard
Box Set: Wings of Earth: Season One
Novella: Scatter the Winds

Short Story
Ghostmaker

WINGS OF EARTH: ONE

ECHOES

OF

STARLIGHT

ERIC MICHAEL CRAIG

Cover Art: Dex Craig of DexFX
Cover Layout: Ducky Smith

PUBLISHED BY

Rivenstone Press

ISBN: 978-1-7337283-2-4

CHAPTER ONE

THE *OLYMPUS DAWN* dropped out of cruise as it passed the outer threshold marker, ten light-hours from Starlight Colony. It was a picture-perfect sub-light transition as the residual photons snapped clear of the ship's hull with the usual flash of infrared that swept up to ultraviolet across the forward screen. From outside, it would have looked like the typical hellish white-light flash of a photon boom, but from the inside, it was a wonderful phototechnic cascade of unimaginable colors.

"All hands rig for space-normal operation." Captain Ethan Walker made the announcement more as a formality than anything else. His small crew had done this hundreds of times, so they knew their jobs. With only a couple exceptions, they'd be snoring and waiting for something interesting to happen.

"You just like the sound of your own voice, don't you?" Nuko Takata said from the seat beside him. When he glanced over, she winked. She'd been his copilot for over two years, and she knew him well enough to understand sarcasm was his preferred language. They had the ConDeck to themselves and she had her legs up and crossed on the corner of the console as she thumbed through the latest newswave on her thinpad.

"Marti, plot a course for the transfer beacon and set speed

to half-light," he said. As the ship's resident Artificial Awareness, Marti did most of the real piloting and at least it wouldn't give him any lip. Usually.

"There is a problem with that, Captain," the AA said in its rich contralto voice. "The beacon seems to be down."

"Down?" Nuko asked. Dropping her feet to the deck, she tossed her screen to the side and leaned forward to look at her console. "It could be in eclipse, but the nav-time says that won't happen for another sixteen hours."

Starlight and its co-orbiting sister planet Shadetree were some of the earliest exoplanets discovered by an old sky survey system that used transiting observation to find worlds orbiting distant stars. Kepler 186 was 178 parsecs from Zone One, but its stellar plane lined up with Earth, so a ship coming in on a direct line from the home system might catch the worlds lined up with each other. When that happened, they'd have no beacon to use to get a navigational fix. The colony's beacon sat at the barycenter of the binary planet and winked out for almost an hour out of every forty-eight.

"You're sure we're in the right system?" he asked, poking at her. She wasn't the navigator, but since she'd punched the buttons last, it had to be her mistake.

"If it's Tuesday, this has to be Starlight," she said, shaking her head.

"It is Kepler 186," Marti said. "I have located the other threshold markers and they triangulate to a high degree of certainty."

"This is a dinky red-dwarf, so let's point our nose down-system and make feet. I'm sure we can find a binary planet within twenty million klick of the big glowing thing down there," he said, not wanting to waste a lot of time digging up problems that might have an easier explanation. "Maybe they've blown a fuse and they're waiting for us to deliver parts."

"Should I try to raise someone on the long-comm?" Nuko asked.

"Let's give them a chance to come out of the shadow and see if the beacon reappears," he said, standing up and shrugging. "We don't want to sound like noobs to the locals, in case it's nothing. Maybe we're reading an old chart that somebody forgot to update and we've got our times off."

"We do not run interstellar navigation on charts," Marti said. "They are inefficient and inaccurate."

"They did when I was in school," he said, rolling his eyes and grinning.

"Improbable, Captain," Marti said.

"Nuko, hold the deck down. I'm thinking I need a little time out of the seat." He turned and headed for the door.

"Sure thing, Boss," she said. "I'll scream when we catch the beacon, and in the middle-time we'll set a course ... that way." She waved a hand in the general direction of the dim red star in front of them.

"Lock it in and make feet," he said over his shoulder as he headed out in search of a meal and some time off the deck. It was his ship, at least on paper, so he took the majority of the time on duty, but after three years running consignment cargo to pay his license and lease, it was getting skinny around the edges.

The door hadn't completely closed behind him when one of the two passengers on this run ambushed him. "Are we there yet?" she said, grinning as his face dropped into a stony glare.

Dr. Keira Caldwell was in her mid-thirties and was the type he once would have chased to ground, although for some reason he knew she was beyond his orbit. There was something about her that told him she didn't breathe the same air he did. She was casual and friendly in an easy sort of way, yet it had a hint of

3

a studied edge to it. He couldn't tell for sure, but he suspected she had money somewhere in her tree. "It's just been a while since I was home and when I heard that we were back down from cruising speed, I figured we were close enough to the end to ask," she said.

"Actually Doctor, we've still a little over twenty hours to go," he said, trying to slip past her in the narrow corridor.

"Twenty-three days on this ship and you still won't call me by my name," she said, winking and shaking her head as she dropped into position and walked with him back toward the lift.

"Sorry… Kaycee. Force of habit," he lied, shrugging. He knew it was safer to keep the wall of propriety firmly in place with her. "We have to drop out of cruise far enough from a star to be outside the clutter. Unfortunately, that means it's crawling speed from here. We're still eleven billion klick from a parking orbit."

"Is there any chance I can comm with the colony before we get there?"

"Yah, you can send a message, but since we're running at half-light, and there's about twenty hours of comm loop time, we'll almost be there by the time you'd get anything back." That was a slight exaggeration but since he didn't see a need to authorize the comm time, he let his oversimplification stand.

"What about the deep-comm?" she asked. "I know it takes a lot of energy, but at this range it isn't too bad is it?"

Stopping at the rail edge, he waited for the lift and twisted to study her face. "Is there something urgent that I need to know about?" After several seconds he realized he was staring at her and his mind had gone into standby. She was a paying passenger, and he was just the hired help, so it was doubly dangerous that something about her tempted his eyes to wander, along with his thoughts.

"Not really," she said. "It's just that I need to make sure they've got a cargo lander waiting at the transfer station. The payload is a bit delicate, and if you're running a tight turnaround, I don't want you to be held up, or to drop and dart leaving us free-floating while we wait on the down-leg."

"I don't have a problem with giving you the comm time, but Starlight's transponder is in eclipse at the moment so it can't be for a while yet," he said. "Since deep-comm runs through the same relay as the beacon, we've got no link to the colony until it comes back into line-of-sight."

"So, it could be as much as an hour before we can downlink." She frowned.

"We're not tight, anyway. We came in about ten percent hot, so we'll make station early," he said. "If you're worried about the environment of the transfer, why didn't you have us contract the downside handling? Nuko's an artist with the drop-ship loader."

"That's good to know," she said, stepping onto the lift platform once the rail opened. "Unfortunately, I didn't arrange that side of the contract and your Cargo Compliance Controller doesn't seem like she'd be much inclined to look the other way and let me make you a side offer."

He followed her into the small cage, and they started down. "Leigh is a good Triple-C, but she does tend to be somewhat ..." he stopped, trying to find a diplomatic way to finish his thought without overstating his opinion.

"The phrase you are looking for is, *tight assed*," she said, winking. "I bet when she breaks wind, dogs come running."

Walker's mouth fell open. He blinked several times as he looked down at the deck and struggled not to laugh. "*Rigid* was the word I was thinking," he said.

Leigh Salazar was a corporate enforcer and responsible for making sure they executed the transport contract from end-to-end on any run they accepted. It meant she was as inflexible as an iron-bar. He didn't particularly like her, but she was the legal agent for the load, and she was excellent at her job.

"Regardless, I didn't even think to ask her because I know what she'd say," Kaycee said.

The railing opened, and they stepped out onto the mid-deck. The majority of the deck was an open space that served as the dining room and recreation area. Because the *Olympus Dawn* also carried passengers, the area was much larger than it needed to be for the crew alone. Captain Walker spotted his Triple-C sitting alone at a table across the room and nodded, making sure Kaycee caught the significant tilt of his head and the warning to change the trajectory of their conversation. Leigh glanced up but paid them no attention. She appeared to be busy reading her morning newswave while she munched on what looked like a brick of yeastcake.

Lowering his voice, he asked, "Do you want me to ask her if she'd be willing to let us make the landing leg for you?"

"Can we feel that out and keep it as a backup in case there isn't a cargo lander available?" she asked.

"Cando," he said. "I'll poke the bear and see if she might be willing to dance."

"Kaycee, may I have a word with you?" Elias Pruitt said as he angled across the deck in their direction from the workout room. He was the other passenger on this run. Wearing a thinskin, he looked more like a two-meter slab of bodyguard flesh than the biomedical systems engineer he was. He was traveling back to Starlight from a vacation at New Hope City and had boarded before they picked up their cargo modules and the doctor at Armstrong Station. Their boarding passes said they weren't traveling together, but they seemed suspiciously casual.

"I'll go grab a meal and will let you know when Nuko says we've got the beacon back," he said, nodding at Elias and ducking out of their conversation.

"The beacon is down?" the engineer asked.

"It's probably in the shadow of—"

"No, sir," he said, glancing at his chrono and shaking his head. "I've been running on Starlight local time since we left Zone One. It's got another fifteen hours and forty-eight minutes."

"Angular position of the planet in orbit relative to our position would change the time," the captain said.

"I know, but that should be very close to right," he said.

"You're probably right," Walker said, trying to play it off with a shrug. "Then they might have it offline for maintenance."

"That would be possible, but don't they send out advisories through FleetCom?" Elias challenged, his dark eyes flashing between the captain and Kaycee.

"They do, but sometimes those don't make it this far down the deck-list," he said, holding up his finger and tapping into his collar comm. "Nuko, have we received a FleetCom advisory on a maintenance cycle on the Kepler 186 beacon?"

"Negative, Captain," Marti answered for her. "There have been no updates to the beacon schedule."

"Yah, Boss can you come back to the ConDeck?" Nuko asked. He knew her well enough to recognize the stress in her voice even if it was undetectable to anyone else. He immediately regretted having used the open comm rather than the command channel. It meant that anyone in earshot was listening in on what she said.

"What's swinging?"

"The beacon isn't in eclipse, it's hard down," she said.

"Down, as in for maintenance," he offered.

"No."

He turned toward the lift and realized both his passengers were following on his heels. "You're obviously saying something else here. Connect the dots for me," he said, trying to figure out a diplomatic way to tell them to wait here. Nothing came quickly to mind, so he tried to ignore them instead.

"Marti used the main navscan dish to boost the sensors, and as far as we can tell, everything else on Starlight is offline too," she said.

"The colony is offline?" Elias asked.

Walker had reached the railing on the lift cage and was hoping that if he stopped there and waited, they wouldn't follow him to the ConDeck. "What does that mean?"

"There are no RF signals anywhere on the surface," Marti said. "There are also no automated comm signals between the orbitals and the ground."

"We can't even detect EM from the power grid," Nuko added.

"Can you tell if something's happened to the colony?" the captain asked.

"Not from this range," she said.

"I'm on my way," he said.

CHAPTER TWO

THE CAPTAIN STOOD behind the empty pilot's seat staring at the screen as they eased into position at the barycenter between the two worlds. Marti and Nuko were flying the ship, so he just watched. Normally seeing two Earth sized planets this close together would be a sight he'd want to enjoy, but the strangeness of the silence stole the pleasure from the moment.

To port, Shadetree was three-quarters illuminated, a blistered red wasteland of scorched barren rock, and to starboard, Starlight was a mottled brown and gray desert with nearly iridescent thin clouds along the poles. Most of its surface was dark and only visible in the reflected light of its companion world.

"We should be able to see the lights of the colony from here," Kaycee said. She sat beside Elias in one of the observation jump seats along the back wall of the ConDeck.

Walker had allowed both of his passengers to stay on the ConDeck as they made their approach, and for the most part, she had spent the time whispering with Pruitt. When Ethan glanced over his shoulder, he could see she was chewing on a big ball of acid. "It could be clouds obscuring the light," he offered.

She shook her head. "It's an ultra-arid desert. Way too hot for heavy clouds."

"The power has to be off," Elias added.

"I would concur with his assessment, Captain," Marti said.

"And I'm sure they'd have backup systems," Nuko said. "There'd be medical centers with emergency generators and who knows what else. There should be some light somewhere down there."

"What could take out the entire power-grid?" Walker asked, swiveling his seat and sitting down. He scratched at his chin while he thought.

"I'm not a power systems engineer, but nothing I know of would do it," Pruitt said.

"Kepler 186 is a red dwarf. They tend to burn their fuel slowly, but sometimes they burp hard." Renford Pascalle was the ship systems engineer, but he was also an armchair astronomer, so that made him the closest thing they had to a science officer. "As tight in as these planets orbit, it might not take much of a solar flare to blast the surface in a big way."

"Rene's got a point. That would also take out the beacon," Nuko said, nodding.

He shook his head. "Someone might have shut it down on purpose, but not because of a flare. All space-based systems use broadcast power distribution and have for the last seventy years. Those beacons use narrow-bandwidth filtering that makes them impervious to surge."

"A stellar eruption of that magnitude would also leave detectable background radiation across wide areas of the star system for weeks," Marti said. "We would have picked it up when we made our approach."

"I assume that means you didn't observe any?" the captain asked.

"Correct," the AA said. "The background stellar winds are normal. There is no detectable evidence of a recent coronal mass ejection."

"That's probably a good thing, since an incident that powerful would have affected people on the surface," Rene said.

"Are there any life signs?" Kaycee asked.

"We're not a science vessel," Ethan said, shaking his head. "Our sensor kit isn't tooled to scan for biosigns. We can pick out the electromagnetic signature of a ship at a distance of better than a light year, and we've got high-end optics to go with that, but otherwise we can't do much beyond sniffing out a base level atmospheric analysis. Spiffs like fancy sensors are a pointless upgrade on a cargo hauler."

Her eyes flashed for an instant before she visibly bit down on whatever had sparked her. Instead she just nodded.

"If it was a flare, they'd all be in the shelters anyway," Elias said. He reached out and squeezed her hand. She jerked her arm free and glared. She didn't appear to be in the mood for his reassurance.

"Shelters?" Nuko asked, making sure that Ethan registered that she'd noticed the strange interaction too.

"There are shelters under the community center buildings and all the major outlying facilities," Kaycee said. "When they planned out the colony, the designers accounted for space weather possibilities."

"Would these shelters be shielded?" Marti asked.

"I don't know," she said, glancing at Elias.

"I am sure they would be," Rene confirmed, although his voice sounded less than confident. "A few meters of soil would be enough for all but the most intense issues." He drummed his fingers on the edge of his control station for several seconds while he chewed over the possibilities. "If the shelters did have extra heavy shielding, that could explain the lack of RF and EM."

"So, they might just be hiding out." Kaycee nodded.

"Don't you think they'd have stuck their heads up to look around and turn the lights back on by now?" the captain said. "If this happened long enough ago that the stellar background levels have returned to normal, they've been holed-up for a while."

"How long could it have been?" Nuko asked.

"When was the last time either of you had any comm with the colony?" Ethan asked.

"I received a message from my family the day before I boarded," Elias said.

"And I sent one from Armstrong Station, the day we got the cargo loaded," the doctor said.

"I don't remember linking one back to you after we made way," Nuko said.

Kaycee shook her head.

"It's more than a six-day transmission delay from Zone One to here," Ethan said. "If we assume the reason you never got a reply was because they were already hiding in the shelters, then the window of this happening is no less than seventeen days ago."

"And based on my message it can't be more than thirty days ago," Elias said. He unfolded from his chair and paced along the upper platform of the ConDeck.

"I don't know how long they'd have supplies in the shelters," Kaycee said. "Probably not much longer than a month, best case."

"That would be my thinking too," Elias said, nodding.

"We need to get down there," she said.

"Before I can possibly say yes to that, we need to know what's going on," the captain said, shaking his head. "What other explanations could knock the entire colony offline?"

"And the beacon," Nuko added.

He nodded. "And the beacon."

"Wager would be it has to be massive hardware failure, and

not something biological," Rene said. "Equipment keeps working even without people to notice."

"If a robot works in a forest and there's no one around to hear it …" Ethan said.

"It still keeps making noise," the engineer finished. "That leans me into the idea that somebody shut it all down."

"But why?" Elias asked, stopping at the end of one of his orbits and glaring at the room in general.

"That brings us back to going down there," Kaycee said, standing up like she meant to leave immediately. "How soon can we—"

"*We* can't," the captain said. "I would be willing to go down and take a look around, but you are paying passengers and that means I'm responsible to keep you safe until we officially arrive at our destination."

"You are fragging joking, aren't you?" she asked, glancing at Nuko and Rene as if to make sure he wasn't serious. "We're here. This is the destination we contracted."

"No," he said, watching Elias focus his glare in his direction. "Until my Triple-C declares the contract complete, I can't let you go down there even if I wanted to."

"That's absurd," she said.

"I'm sure it feels that way to you," he said, shrugging. "Leigh has to make the call and I'm certain she will not waive the liability clause in your transport contracts until we're sure there's nothing dangerous happening on the surface."

"Captain Walker, you cannot be saying you will hold us here against our will," Elias said, enunciating every word making him sound more menacing than he already was. "This is our home. We have rights under Coalition law and you really don't want to be crossing that line, considering how that would go for you."

"If you want to take this up with Leigh Salazar, I am sure she'll explain the legality, and my rights to make this call," he said.

"I will do that," he said, his voice descending toward a growl. Pivoting, he disappeared through the door.

"Ethan, please," Kaycee said. "He's right, this is our home. We've both got family in the colony."

"I understand that, but I just can't," he said. "I know that's frakked, but I have to put your safety first."

She shook her head. "My whole life is down there. It's everything I've spent my life working on. You can't seriously expect me to sit here and wait."

"I'm sorry Doctor, but that is exactly what I expect you to do," he said, trying to sound firm. "You're welcome to stay here on the ConDeck and monitor the situation as long as you don't do anything to countermand my instructions to Nuko."

"But—"

"Or you can go talk to my Triple-C and see how truly inflexible she can be," he said. "The choice is yours."

Turning his back on her he stepped over to Nuko. "Let Leigh know Pruitt's on his way to twist her arm, and that I already explained the answer to him." He leaned forward and lowered his voice. "The ship is yours. Under no circumstances are you to let either of them push you into anything, nor are you to let them distract you. I don't know what we're going to find down there, but it stinks hard. I want the best possible assessment of what I'm up against once we land."

"Yah, Boss. Cando," she said. "Then you are going down?"

He nodded.

"Leigh's not going to like that, either," she said.

"It's a no-risk excursion," he said. "Not likely to be a biohazard, so she can't get too bent."

"Hopefully." She shrugged. "It's your skin, but she is a Triple-C so it's a fair odds guess how her brain works."

Squeezing her shoulder, he winked. "Marti, saddle up one of your walkabouts with good eyes and load it into shuttle-one," he said. "Rene, you're with me."

"We ought to take Preston too," the engineer suggested, getting up and heading toward the door. He paused to wait for an answer before leaving.

"Your med-tech?" Kaycee said. "Take me. I'm a lot better qualified than Reed is, and I know the layout of the colony."

"That may be true on both counts, but we've already covered this and I won't risk letting you go down there until we know what's going on," he said, turning toward her and crossing his arms as he studied her face. "You want to do something? Sit down at one of the consoles and help Nuko and Marti figure out what we might be looking at. It's probably nothing, but I don't want to have my eggs hanging in the wind."

"I'd be better with eyes on the ground beside you," she said.

He closed his eyes and shook his head. She just wasn't going to give it up. "We'll maintain a constant optic channel on the comm, and you'll be able to watch every move we make. It'll almost be as good as being there with us."

She sighed but nodded and took the engineer's vacant seat. "You'll need to move fast once you get on the surface," she said. "I'm not used to the view from orbit, but the sun looks to be close to coming up."

"Local sunrise is in thirteen minutes," Marti confirmed. "Transit time to the landing center is fifty-seven minutes."

"It's important for you to remember Starlight's an extreme desert," she explained. "It will be twenty to thirty centigrade as the sun comes up, but because the air is so dry, it heats fast. Within an hour of sunrise, it will be forty-five. By morning dark, it will be over fifty. It's a pity that you can't make it down there before sunrise."

He whistled. "Morning dark?"

"There's almost an hour of eclipse every day-cycle as the colony passes through the shadow of Shadetree. It cools things off a little and you get some amazing views of the inner planets and the stars, but when the sun comes out from behind the other planet it gets hotter than frak before nightfall."

"'*Hotter than frak*' means what?" he asked.

"Over sixty centigrade," she said. "You can survive that outside for a short time if you're used to it. But you aren't and won't. Honestly, don't even plan to try. If the power really is down, there will be no climate control in any of the buildings, so you're better off staying in the shade outside where the breeze will help. But you really need to be back aboard your shuttle before the eclipse ends if you can."

"Will the environmental controls in an EVA suit keep us from baking?" he asked, turning to Rene who was still standing by the door and looked like he'd already started sweating. For practice.

He shook his head. "It might for a little while, but I don't think so. The cooling in a standard suit isn't designed to unload heat into an environment that hot."

"That means no on the EVA suits," Walker said, frowning.

"The air is ultra-dry, so evaporation is your friend," Kaycee said. "If you get into a crisis, you can soak your clothes with water and that will cool you off some. It won't be comfortable, but it will buy you some extra time if you need it."

"Is there anything else we need to worry about?" the captain asked. "Maybe giant worms that poop purple poison or something?"

"You have to watch out for your eyes," she said. "The light is only about ninety percent as bright as Earth's sun, but it's heavy on the low red end of the visible spectrum. It carries a lot more energy than it looks like it does, but what you have to realize is that when your eyes start hurting, you need to get into deep shade and give them a chance to rest. If you don't, you will get what we call ocular migraines, and they can be crippling."

"How long does it take to get to that point?" Rene asked.

"You'll have at least a half day-cycle outside, give or take," she said, shrugging. "Some people are more susceptible than others. A mild headache will be the first symptom that you're getting into trouble. Your eyes aren't designed to focus the red wavelength light, so they have to strain to see clearly. You might not feel it coming on until you've reached the point of being in trouble, either. You'll need to pay close attention."

"Will EVA suit visors help?" Rene asked. "I could jiffy-rig something."

"A bit," she said. "They design most suit helmets to filter out the blue spectrum light since it damages the eyes faster, but it would be better than nothing. If you can get your hands on the local eyewear, it provides much better protection against chromatic aberration, and will keep you from going sky-blind right away."

"Starlight sounds like such a wonderful place," Walker said. "Why the hell would anyone build a colony here?"

CHAPTER THREE

SLICING DOWN THROUGH THE ATMOSPHERE, Captain Walker manually piloted the shuttle. If this had been a routine landing, he'd have let Marti drive them to the landing center, but he wanted to make a fast pass over the colony on the way down, and if he sat in the nose chair he'd get the best view. Preston and Rene sat in the seats behind him and stared out the side windows looking for any signs of life.

He made a low approach and banked hard around a small ridge that protected the landing pads from what looked like an endless sea of sand. Without approach control markers to help him navigate, he almost overshot the terminal before he snapped into a stern-flip and dropped down hard toward the landing apron.

The sun was three hours above the horizon and shadows arced across the landscape. Even from a thousand meters, they could see heat waves shimmering off any surface exposed to the direct sunlight.

Angling the shuttle toward the shadow of the loop tube, he remembered Kaycee's warning. If he wanted to be able to touch the door mechanism to get back in, he'd need to park out of the sunlight if possible. She said the locals called it the art of shade conservation.

"What do you notice?" Ethan asked as he extended the gear and made his final descent.

"That it already looks hot?" Preston said.

"Of course, it looks hot. You're from Mars. Everything looks hot to you," Rene said.

"No, look around," the captain said. "What don't you see that you should?"

"People? But Kaycee said it's hot, so they'd all be inside," the med-tech said.

"That's not what I'm talking about. Where are the landers?"

"It's hot," he said again. "Maybe they keep them in hangars.

Ethan rolled his eyes and sighed. "That's possible, but do you see any hangar buildings?"

"No, but it's hot. Maybe they're underground."

Walker glared hard enough it bounced off the forward window and almost flattened Preston in his seat. He heard him flinch, or maybe it was Rene trying not to laugh.

"What about it, Kaycee?" he asked as he cut power and let the shuttle settle on the tarmac. "Are there underground hangars?"

"I've been studying at Armstrong for a while," she said, coming back over the comm. "When I left, I hadn't heard anything about plans for underground hangers."

"Then where are all the ships?" he asked.

"There should be at least a squadron of orbital transports," Rene said.

"Maybe a couple pleasure-craft, too," Ethan said. You did say there were some affluent families here, didn't you?"

"Yah," she confirmed.

"Is there somewhere else they'd have parked them?" he asked.

"There are mining operations scattered all over the hemisphere, but most of them are small," she said.

"And no other cities?" Rene asked.

"This is the only one with a landing center," she said.

"There's been no comm from the tower either," the captain said, swinging around and standing up in the small cabin.

"You didn't expect any did you?" Rene asked.

"No, but I don't like this. I didn't see anything moving on the flyover, did you two?"

They both shook their heads.

"We've also got no one coming out to say hello," Ethan said. "It's not like they wouldn't have seen us coming in."

When the outer door of the lock opened, and the first blast of hot air washed over them, even Walker gasped in shock. He glared at Preston before he had a chance to say it again.

"Marti, are you ready to unpack your skin?"

"Standing by for you to vacate the airlock, Captain," it said. "Until you go outside, there isn't room for me to join you."

Let's do this," Walker said, grabbing a visor out of the tool locker and slipping the band over his head. He jumped down to the surface and flipped the faceplate down. A small heads-up linked him to one of the optics on Marti's automech and he blinked in surprise. "Nice touch Rene."

"I grabbed the whole comm-kit when I jerked the visors out of the EVA suit helmets," the engineer said. "I figured it would be nice to share integrated communications if things get sticky."

"You don't mind us riding parasite on your eyes, do you Marti?"

"Of course not, Captain," Marti said over both the comm and through the audio on its body simultaneously.

Walker spun around in time to watch the mechanical extension of the AA unlimber itself as it emerged through the airlock and onto the ground. Marti had a collection of bodies to choose from since it spent the majority of its share of their earnings on new personal hardware.

As it unfolded its legs and stood up, it bore an uncanny resemblance to a spider fused with a vaguely human shaped torso. It had a teardrop shaped head, mounted on a giraffe neck with a sensor ring that made it look like it was wearing a sombrero.

As far as the captain knew, this was the first time this particular automech had seen use. In fact, since it had already been stored in its holding locker on the shuttle when they'd boarded, he'd not seen it before at all.

"Is that a Gendyne 6000?" he asked as he watched the four arms rotate around on their control rings to what he assumed to be the front of the body. "When did you pick this one up?"

"I acquired it during our last maintenance at Alpha Five," it said. Marti's usual female voice sounded more than a little disconcerting coming from this mechanical behemoth. "There was a robotics distributor there when we arrived, and I got an exceptional deal. They included the two extra-fine motor manipulators and the extended sensor kit in the base price, so I could not resist."

"Sweet beans," Preston said. "But can we talk about your sexy hardware later? If you don't mind, I'd like to get inside somewhere cool. I think my earwax is melting."

"Marti, let's do a quick scan here first and then we'll pick our target," Walker said. "Do you have bio-sign gear on that fancy rig of yours?"

"I do," Marti said, extending its legs out to form a wide base and telescoping the neck up almost five meters.

"That's a trip," Rene said as he stumbled backward. "Don't watch the optic in full-screen on your visor while the neck is doing that."

"My range on biological detection is less than 1,000 meters, depending on environmental interference," it said. "Inside a structure it might be substantially reduced."

As Walker watched, the screen along the top of his visor rotated, slowly covering a complete 360-degree arc.

"No life-signs detected in range, however the buildings appear to be metal-polymer alloy and will greatly reduce sensor efficiency."

"What about anything else? Audio? Motion? Anything?" he asked as he swung his own circle with his eyes.

"Negative," Marti said. "We appear to be alone."

"Captain Walker, the main passenger concourse is on the other side of the building in front of you," Kaycee said. "The loop tube has a terminal inside there and if anyone is around, that's where they'd be."

"You don't think there'd be any in the tower?" he asked.

"Probably not. I am pretty sure it was all run by AA systems," she said. "They even piloted most of the ships. I don't think there were a handful of qualified shuttle pilots in the whole colony."

"I guess that makes it a better place to start," he said. "Rene, you stay with the shuttle and we'll foot it over and do a looksee."

"I don't like this," the engineer said. "You might need me and if there's nobody around, then there's no reason to post a guard."

"Engineer Pascalle is correct, his skills may be essential in restoring power or other systems," Marti said. "I can maintain a teleoperation link to the shuttle and prevent anyone from stealing it."

"I keep forgetting you can be a thousand places at once," Walker said, nodding.

"Actually, there is a finite number of tasks I can do simultaneously, but my current threshold is well above three," Marti said as it retracted its neck and moved off toward the building. "I do not think protecting the shuttle is a matter that will exceed my capacity."

The far less heat tolerant humans stayed in the shadow of the loop tube as Marti shot across the open space in a strange loping gallop. A gentle breeze kicked up wisps of fine dust as they walked. It only took two minutes to cover the distance, but by the time they got to the ground level entrance they were all covered in sweat.

"The door mechanism is inoperative," Marti said as they approached. "I am detecting no power inside the wall."

"How do we get in then?" Preston said. "I think we need to get out of this heat soon or we'll be in trouble."

"We could cut through the wall and see if we can manually power the door with Marti's power supply," Rene suggested.

"I do have external power adaptors for peripheral systems, so that would be a better solution than breaking a window," it said.

Walker nodded and stepped back to let the automech move into position.

The engineer pointed at where to make the incision while one of the industrial level arms selected a cutting laser from its tool holster. A shower of molten sparks erupted from the wall as it went to work on the outer skin of the building.

"Holy frak, I grew up in Bountiful, so I've never felt heat like this," Preston said as he stepped farther away from the cutting work. "I hate to sound like a whiffer, but this is brutal."

"I thought you were from Mars," Rene said.

"Bountiful is on Mars. It's outside of Lehi City," he said.

"If you say so," he said over his shoulder as he supervised Marti. "You've never been to Earth have you?"

Preston shook his head.

"There were places before they started the geo-engineering projects that were this hot. Probably hotter," he said.

"He's right," Walker said. "On one of my school breaks I got to tour the largest ghost town in North America. It was in the

Great Western Desert. They called the place Phoenix."

"I've never been there, but I've heard of it," Rene said. "It was named after an ancient story of a bird that lit itself on fire in order to be reborn."

"The name fit," the captain said. "In the daytime sun, it was probably over fifty centigrade by mid morning. What I just couldn't believe was that at one point, over twelve million people lived there."

"Why would they build a city in a place like that?" Preston said.

"It wasn't always that bad, but when the environmental collapse started, they had to abandon the city," he said. "Phoenix is now sitting in the middle of an immense wasteland covered in sand and waiting to be reborn."

"It's just sitting empty?" Rene asked as Marti reached in with its second heavy arm and bent the plating off the side of the building so it could access the internal hardware.

"That was what amazed me the most," Walker said. "There were a few thousand people still living there. Apparently, their families had stayed all the way through from before they declared it uninhabitable. They adapted to an almost impossible situation, but humans do that. Even here, they will adapt. I might have chosen a more hospitable place to build a colony, but I have no doubt that they'll endure and prosper. Even on the doorstep of hell."

A sudden explosion of sparks and smoke flashed out of the wall and Marti's automech body reeled back, teetering on stiff legs.

"What the frag?" Rene barked as he slapped at small burning spots in his thin worksuit. A dozen holes had singed their way through to his skin and he was blinking his eyes furiously.

"Marti, are you still with us?" Walker asked as he watched the robot body twitch and shudder.

"I am, although until the servo-interface reboots, I am not able to access my body," the AA said over the comlink from the ship. "I believe the appropriate word is, *ouch*?"

"What happened?" Rene asked. He'd pulled out a handheld multi-scanner and was looking at the screen while he shook his head.

"I attempted to access the primary feed to the door hardware, and there is apparently a dead-to-ground power sink connected to the circuit. When I made the connection, it shorted my limiter out and tried to pull my total power reserve through the connection."

"Yah, it looks like it," Rene said. "It slagged the end of the connector as well as about twenty centimeters of the power conduit in the arm. It's going to be down until we can get you a new piece manufactured."

"A dead-to-ground power sink? Like a short circuit?" the captain asked as he watched the automech body come back online in gradual increments. The legs extended and then flexed one at a time. When that finished, the arms gyrated through several cycles. All of them moved correctly, except the damaged one, and it stuck out like a dead stump.

"I do not believe it was a short," Marti said, its voice reappearing through the automech's audio after the startup cycle had completed. "My connector is protected against that type of fault."

"Then what was it?"

"I do not know for sure," it said. "The sensation was like my power core was being drained directly into a damping field of some type. It was unlike anything I have ever experienced."

"A damping field?" Rene asked.

"Yes. The high and low sides of the circuits were held isolated so that the breakers would not engage, but an infinite load appeared at the connection. It was like being held open and forced to supply power without limit," the AA said. "I lost fifty-five percent of my energy reserves before the connection failed. I was unable to affect any protection against this effect."

"What could cause that?" Ethan asked.

"Unknown."

"Could it be a defensive system of some sort?" Rene asked. "Like a fail-safe locking mechanism."

"Also, unknown."

"So how do we get inside?"

"I no longer have a laser torch in my kit," Marti said. "I could attempt to cut through the wall mechanically to get to the interior. I do have other tools that would be adequate for the task, although they would be slower."

"Mechanically? You mean a saw?" Rene asked.

"Essentially true."

"Then there's a risk you would cut into a conduit that might be connected to this power sink," the engineer said, shaking his head. "If the first short took you down by over half, I don't want to be lugging your metal carcass back to the shuttle."

"Especially in this heat," Preston said, nodding.

"I agree," Walker said. "I'd like to hold off on that idea until we know what we're looking at. If this isn't something that you recognize, then we might be looking at other surprises."

"That is a distinct possibility, Captain."

CHAPTER FOUR

THE WALK TO TOWN would have been unbearable except that Marti's automech had four small platforms, complete with handrails, to stand on. The spider legs could carry them at almost ten kilometers an hour and the relative breeze as they passed through the air was surprisingly refreshing, if they overlooked the fact that the air felt like it was coming out of a smelter furnace. Fortunately, it didn't smell like it.

They followed the loop tube for all but the last kilometer where it disappeared into the ground at the edge of the colony. From there, they stayed as much as possible to the shadow of the low buildings. Unfortunately, the colonists had built the structures on the outskirts of town far apart, so there was little to do but to endure the baking between patches of shade.

Most of the buildings on the edges of the colony were far less sophisticated than the landing center. That meant many of them had manual doors. Every time they approached one, they stopped to walk the perimeter and check for occupants. The first three were industrial warehouses where robotic additive printers stacked manufactured goods for automated pick-up and delivery. Silence echoed back at them when they entered and made it clear that if there had ever been humans who worked inside, they were nowhere to be found.

The further they pressed toward the center of the colony the more certain they were that nobody was around. Nothing moved. Anywhere.

"This is unnerving," Ethan said as he hung on to Marti's body with one arm and used a hand as a shade for his eyes so he could scan the distance.

"This reminds me of the pics I've seen of the Burroughs Museum," Rene said.

"Yah, a bit," Preston said, nodding and not looking up from the handhold in front of him. "Bountiful is in Chryse Planitia. We lived a few hundred klick from the Old Burroughs Dome so I went there a couple times as a kid."

"Really? That's sweet beans. It's a place I've always wanted to visit when I'm in Zone One," Rene said.

"After they invented Omnicyn, it would have been easy to reoccupy the colony. But it never happened," he said, shrugging. "My father thought it was important to remember, but I think he actually did it to scare the jammies off us kids."

"Your dad sounds like a flatch," Walker said.

"I don't think he understood how terrifying the echoes across the promenade were to us kids. My sisters used to have nightmares about it" he said. "I don't know why people didn't move back in, but some crazy old chancellor decided that, as her last act in office, she'd declare it a monument. They pumped it full of nitrogen, and now you have to wear a breathing mask to go in."

"That might be a bit creepifying," Rene said. "At least they cleaned it up before they sealed it."

"True, but what bothers me is that there are no bodies here either," he said. "Who cleaned them up?"

"Hopefully, they're not dead," the captain said, tapping his ear to remind the med-tech that the passengers aboard the *Olympus Dawn* were still listening.

"You're right," the engineer said. "Maybe they've all holed up somewhere and they've managed to keep the power working. Or if they're in an underground shelter, that might be a lot cooler, too."

"The only major shelters are under the buildings in the civic center," Kaycee said, confirming his suspicion that they were still on the line. "And under the hospitals."

"Copy that," Ethan said, shooting Preston a '*told you so*' glare. "We haven't gotten that far. At the rate we're progressing, if we don't skip most of these smaller buildings, we won't get there before it gets too hot to work outside. We'll have to find shelter soon."

"It's been hotter inside the buildings than outside," Preston said.

"That says the power has been down for a while," Elias said. Apparently, he'd had his legal ass handed to him by Leigh. He sounded much less hostile than he had before they left the ship. "The buildings were all built with heavy passive solar resistance. It would take days for them to heat to a point where're they're hotter than the outside. Even with no power, for the heat to have penetrated to that point you're, talking at least a week."

"A residence, Captain," Marti said, slowing down and indicating a building with its one remaining fine motor arm.

"Let's scan it," he said. "With eyeballs."

"I'm detecting no life signs in the structure," the AA said as it stopped at the end of a narrow walkway that ran up to the building.

"I'm not surprised, but let's look around anyway," he said, jumping off the automech platform and kicking up a small cloud of dust as he hit the sidewalk. "There may be some clues as to where they went and why. "Rene, you and Marti see if you can work your way around back and Preston and I will go up to the door."

The med-tech eased himself down to the ground and shook his head while Marti skittered off with the engineer. "Frak, I just can't do this," he groaned as he leaned forward to put his hands on his knees.

"Are you alright?" Ethan asked, leaning down beside him.

He shook his head, then flipped his visor up and squinted toward the building. His skin was dry and red.

"Kaycee are you able to see my personal optic?" the captain asked.

"Yah," she said.

"What am I looking at here?"

"It looks like he's going hyperthermic," she said. His body's not regulating his internal temperature by sweating."

"They don't teach sweating on Mars," Preston said. He tried to straighten up but pitched back. If Walker hadn't been expecting it, he'd have dropped clear over.

"What can I do?" he asked, grabbing the med-tech by his arm and stabilizing him on his feet.

"Get him into shade somewhere and soak him down," she said. "He's got to get cooled off."

"How much time do we have?" he asked, looking around for a place he could get him out of the sun.

"Not a lot," she said, her voice made it clear she was serious.

Looping an arm around Preston, he propped him up and dragged him toward the residence. His legs buckled several times, but they managed to get to the thin strip of shade along the west edge of the building. The wall was hot to the touch, but he leaned him back against it anyway and pulled out his waterbag.

"Should I just pour this over him?" Walker asked.

"Yah, try to make sure you soak as much of his torso and head as possible, and then get air moving over him.

Preston hissed as the water drenched him, blinking several times, and shaking his head like he was drunk. His slowly swinging eyes made it clear he was having trouble thinking, and he drooped back against the wall.

Marti appeared around the corner of the building and skidded to a stop beside them. "I can take him back to the shuttle and then come back for you. With only one passenger I can get him there in eight minutes tops."

"You need to do that," she said. "The shuttle's cool. It will help bring his core temp down."

"I will come back for you as quickly as I can," Marti said, picking the limp med-tech up by the front of the shirt with one of its heavy arms. It swung him into position and anchored him down with the other arm.

"Where's Rene?"

"Waiting outside the back door." The AA switched from audio to the commlink as it spun away at a much higher clip than they had used coming in. "The back door was standing open, and we were about to report to you when the priorities changed."

"Understood," Walker said, glancing at his remaining water supply. Less than a liter left. "We'll recon the house and wait for you to come back for us."

"Copy," Marti said. It was already out of sight except for the cloud of dust that was billowing behind it as it scampered down the road toward the landing center.

Skirting the edge of the building and pushing through a gate into a private yard, he found Rene squatting in the shade of a small bushy tree. It was the first plant they'd seen on Starlight and it was covered with large red brown fruit of some kind.

"So, will he be alright?" he asked as the captain came over

and crawled into the shade beside him.

"I don't know. This is about as far from Mars as you can get. I should have thought about it, but his body isn't going to do as well with the heat."

Rene nodded. He was holding one of the hard-shelled fruit in his hand and rolling it over. "I wonder if this is edible?"

"Yes, it is," Kaycee said. "It's called a pomegranate. The trees grew in arid places on Earth and we brought them here when we first set up the colony because we thought they might adapt well."

"Do you bite through the shell?" he asked.

"No, you break it open and eat the seeds inside. It is juicy and high in vitamin C, and a bunch of other stuff that's good for you," she said. "I haven't had one in a couple years now. I love them."

"How do you know if it's ripe?"

"I always just cracked one open and tasted it. It's tart and a little sweet if it's ripe. Maybe like a cranberry."

"A what?" he asked.

"Don't be a coward, just crack it open and try it."

"I think I'll pass for now," the captain said, plucking two of them and tucking them into his belt pouch.

Rene sighed heavily and made intentional eye contact before he tapped his collar mic to turn off the commlink. He waited for Ethan to follow suit before he said, "I think we might have a body in there."

"Why?"

"Marti's skinsuit doesn't have a sense of smell, but I do," he said, rolling his eyes in a good impression of a person about to lose containment of their last meal. "It's hot in there and that's not a pleasant experience."

"Did you see a body?"

"No. I couldn't push through it," Rene said.

"Got it," the captain said. Taking a deep breath, he rolled back to a standing position and nodded. "You wait here, and I'll go check it out."

"You don't want to do that," the engineer said. "Seriously."

"You're right I don't, but we have to know what's going on here," he said.

"We can wait for Marti to get back," the engineer said. "No sense of smell would be a blessing."

"When it gets back, we're leaving," he said. "I'll just make a quick run in and see. I can hold my breath for a minute at least."

"You really don't want to do that," Rene said. "It could be something contagious."

"If it is, we've already been exposed," Ethan said. Looking around, he started toward the house.

He'd covered about half the distance to the back door when the wall of reek slammed him in the face and he thought about turning back. It was definitely rotting flesh.

Gulping in a deep breath and swallowing hard, he launched himself through the door, and into what looked like a galley. It was clean and dark. And sweltering hot. Painfully, oppressively, hot.

Across the room, he could see another doorway and he pushed toward it. Pulling out his handbeam, he switched it on. His eyes were burning, and he wanted to gasp, but he knew that if he did, he'd be doomed.

Rounding a corner and driving himself deeper into a narrow hallway, he tried to figure out where he should go. There were several doors to the sides and a bigger area straight ahead. *Where would a person go to die? Alone, or with the whole family?*

He opted for the big room and as soon as he entered it, he saw the source of the smell.

The dining table.

Sitting in the middle of the table was what had probably been a family dinner. Protein slabs and yeastcakes and some kind of rich brown stuff. Maybe it had been gravy once.

It was not a dead body. It was dinner. A week or more ago.

He let out a sigh of relief and then realized his mistake. *It meant he had to breathe in.*

Spinning around, he raced back in the direction he'd come, retracing his steps double fast, until he burst out into the air. Gulping down a deep lungful of scalding hot air, he knew instantly that he was still too close to the door. The smell at this range was a vile taste, and he fought to not topple over and retch. Stumbling across the yard toward the tree, he crashed down, gasping. Rene grabbed him by the shoulders and hauled him the rest of the way into the shadow.

"Holy mother of Fred, you stink," he said. "Frag, I hope you didn't get any on me. Please tell me it isn't contagious."

"It isn't," Walker said. "I think it was meatloaf."

"Meatloaf?"

"Yah. No dead bodies," he said, chuffing out his breath and almost laughing. He rolled over onto his back and nodded. The ground was hot, but an odd cool breeze had kicked up and it felt refreshingly not hellish. "It was rotting food."

"Ah, the refrigeration was out in the galley." The engineer nodded. "That makes sense. A cold locker with a bad door—"

"No, it was dinner sitting on a table and dished up on plates," the captain said. "Some of it might have been half-eaten already, but I didn't want to stick around and check."

"Eaten by what?"

"By the family that lived here. It looks like they sat their eating tools down and vanished." He shook his head. "It doesn't even look like they left in a particular rush. Everything seemed to be in place."

"People don't just disappear," Rene said.

"You want to go in and look for yourself?" he challenged.

"No."

"Then I recommend you lay back and enjoy the show." He pointed up just as the sun winked out and the stars spread across the sky in a wave.

To someone that worked on a starship the view wasn't spectacular, but for some unexplained reason, the darkness had a sinister edge that made him shiver in a most decidedly bone-chilling way.

Fortunately, Marti was due back in a few minutes and then they could get back to the ship.

CHAPTER FIVE

WHEN THE SHUTTLE DOCKED, Kaycee, Leigh, and Elias had all crowded into the hangar deck's small observation room. The ship's two cargo handlers also hung back to both sides of the lift cage. Ostensibly they were here to lend a hand, but the truth is they were standing by to keep the two passengers from going hyperbolic and starting a problem.

On paper Billiam Chandler and Angelique Wolfe had signed on to the *Olympus Dawn* to process and load cargo, although with the recent upsurge in deep space piracy Cochran Space had cross trained all their handlers in security ops. That meant they were on board to deal with trouble more than to wrestle crates. They both looked the part of hired muscle even when they were trying to be unobtrusive.

Preston stood propped between Rene and Ethan when they emerged through the shuttle airlock and Kaycee reached out to take his arm. "Let me get him on ice in the MedBay first and then we can go over what you found out."

"You don't need to do that," the captain said, nodding to Wolfe to come and get him. "We can take care of him, and you're a passenger."

"I'm a doctor first," she said, fixing him with an expression that left little doubt that she didn't intend to argue over propriety.

Leigh protested. "But you might be—"

Kaycee spun so fast toward her that the Triple-C took a step back. The air around her froze, and she nodded meekly. Rene snickered, and the captain fixed him with a laser eyeball of his own. It wasn't often that someone could put Leigh in her place, especially without a word.

"Like I said, Elias and I will get his hyperthermic stress stabilized, and then we'll come talk to you," Kaycee said, turning back to the captain and shooting him a conspiratorial wink.

"I think I'll be alright," Preston said.

"Probably, but let's make sure," she said as the two of them led him toward the lift. The handlers both squeezed in behind them.

"Did Nuko order that?"

"She suggested that Mr. Pruitt could be a handful if he became agitated, and that it might be prudent to have them provide an escort any time they were in the command sections of the ship," Marti said.

"Has he given anyone a problem?"

"Me," Leigh said.

"I think he meant people, so you don't count," Rene said, slapping his hand over his mouth and jumping behind the captain. "Oops, sorry."

"Why don't you go deal with machinery or something," she said, firing off a melodramatic glare in his direction. Rene was the only one on the ship that seemed to have a real friendship with her, even if it was a bit odd at times.

"That's a good idea," Ethan said. "See if you can help Marti repair the damaged arm on its skinsuit. We might need to go back down there, and I'd like it to be back in spec if we do."

"You both need to shower," she said, wrinkling up her nose. "But first Ethan, if I may have a word with you? In my office?"

"You're in trouble now," Rene said as he swung around and ducked back into the shuttle to grab his toolkit and the arm section he'd removed from Marti's automech.

"*First*, I need to file a report to FleetCom," he said. "If you want to follow me to my wardroom, we can talk once I am done with that."

"I'll give you a few minutes to take care of that, and maybe to scrape off some of the reek, and then I'll be there," she said. "I think perhaps I need to refresh your memory on what you can, and cannot, do as a lease carrier for CSL. Your obligation is to the cargo first, and that needs to direct your actions from here forward."

She pivoted as the lift returned to the deck, leaving him staring after her and chewing on his lip.

"You can't let her get to you," Rene said, returning with his toolkit. "She's doing her job, and honestly she's not as bad as some I've crewed with in the past."

"I know you're right." The captain nodded, letting out a long slow breath. "Go shower man, you stink."

"You should talk. I'm not the one that charged into the fog of eternal stench. You smell like dead things."

"It was frakking meatloaf!" he said as he grabbed the next lift run and headed up to the crewdeck and his quarters.

∞

The shower helped a lot, both in removing the malodorous layer of sweat and grime, and in giving him time to sort his thoughts. He still had no idea what was going on down on the surface, but he knew it wasn't something that would work itself out without more information. Unfortunately, it also wasn't a situation he had the tools to deal with. He realized that much, even without answering the hundred questions that were chewing on him.

"Marti, where's the nearest FleetCom center?" he asked as he dropped into his seat and drummed his fingers on the edge of his console.

"Cygnus Deep-Three is 15.9 parsecs. Transmission time one way is thirteen hours and fifty-five minutes."

"Spin up the comm," he said, watching the display as the FTL transmitter powered up. When the icon blinked ready, he cleared his throat and tapped the screen to record his message.

"Cygnus Deep-Three, this is Ethan Walker, Captain M-9–2710-HCO of the CSV-1070 Lease Transport *Olympus Dawn*. Our current position is Kepler 186e Starlight, Cygnus.

"Please be advised that we arrived at Starlight Colony and need to report an unknown incident has occurred on the surface. It appears the colony may have suffered some form of catastrophic event. When we arrived, we were unable to make contact with automated approach systems and discovered the colony itself is experiencing an ongoing systemic failure of its infrastructure. Within the limitations of our sensor capabilities, we can detect no signs of activity anywhere in the K-186 system.

"We have undertaken a limited excursion to the surface. While on the surface we did not make contact with anyone, nor did we find any evidence of mass casualties. Prior to returning to the ship we observed standard bio-hazard protocols and have detected no contamination from our limited exposure.

"Passengers aboard the *Olympus Dawn* are concerned that any response to this situation may be time critical, as the colony is fundamentally dependent upon technological support for basic survival.

"We will maintain position at the Starlight Colony transfer beacon and await release, or further instruction.

"Walker, Commander *Olympus Dawn*. Out."

He tapped the icon again to review the transcript of the message and nodded. "Formal enough sounding I guess," he said out loud. "Attach what we know so far and send it."

"Message away," the AA said. "Leigh Salazar is approaching your office."

"Wonderful," he said, sighing as he closed the comm and waited for her to rap on his door. She came in and sat down.

"I know officially you've got to do this, but can we just keep it in perspective please?" he said. He was in no mood for her bureaucratic finger-wagging in spite of the fact that she had the right, and obligation, to pull him up short when he got out of line. The company line anyway.

"Perspective is an interesting choice of word Ethan," she said. She only used his first name when she was about to lecture him on his miniscule place in the universe. She was younger than he was, but she reminded him of his mother when she started out with his name. "From my perspective you've put the cargo in jeopardy."

Normally she wasn't difficult to deal with, but he could tell she thought he'd done something monumentally stupid. Her job was to protect the passengers and cargo in a legal sense, and anytime anything unexpected came up, she had to do her best to mitigate the risk side of the situation. The unknown that they'd encountered had to represent an uncontrollable variable in her mind.

"I know my job and I'm good at it," he said. "I've got the best performance record in the CSL lease fleet. I've never lost a load for failing to deliver and you know that."

"Yes, I do." She nodded. "Unfortunately, that doesn't change the facts. You took unnecessary chances with the cargo and your passengers by going down there to investigate. The

Olympus Dawn may be a slick new rig, but you aren't mastering a multicruiser. You don't have a staff of scientists to figure things out. You don't even have a real ship doctor. How do you know you aren't stepping into something dangerous?"

"Why do you think I am?" he challenged. "Without looking around, we don't have any way to even guess." It was a weak defense for his actions and he knew it, but she had made him feel like he had to push back.

"You're right. There isn't any way to know." She leaned forward and put her elbows on the arms of her chair and laced her fingers in front of her chin. "You're not qualified to guess, but that's exactly why you can't afford to do that. What if the reason you're not getting a reply is because they all ended up with something contagious? It could be something deadly, like the disease that killed Burroughs."

"You're being alarmist. There are no bodies down there," he said. *But Preston and Rene had picked up on that same feeling, too.*

"You mean there are no bodies you've found, *so far*," she said. "That doesn't mean there aren't piles of dead packed away somewhere."

"There's nothing down there."

"Did you look in a hospital?" she challenged. "Did you make it that far?"

"No," he said. "Preston went down before we did."

"That's probably a good thing," she snapped. "The sickest place on a planet is the hospital. If you'd gotten that far and it was a virus, you'd damned sure have brought it here. We'd all be infected right now." She shook her head. "For that matter, we might already be, and just not know it yet."

"We ran a med sweep in the shuttle before we came back to the ship," he said. "It's part of why we took so long getting up from the surface."

"So maybe you got lucky this time," she said. "But there's no way you can say your actions were protecting the cargo. Or the passengers. Right now, you've got a crew member in MedBay being tended to by a paying passenger."

She paused and shook her head. "That's a whole extra glueball right there. The company will have to figure out how to compensate her for taking care of staff personnel who were injured on duty. You risked your crew, and everything else, just to satisfy your curiosity."

"It wasn't about curiosity," he lied. "I'm trying to make a delivery. I can't do that if I don't locate someone to take custody of the shipment. Going down there might have been the only way to have solved that problem."

"That's a thin excuse and you know it," she said, calling him on it with a frown.

"It's not an excuse, it's the truth." He held his hand up to cut off another volley. "The point is, I've had to bring FleetCom in on this now. I don't know what's going on down there, but it does require that I alert the authorities." He stood up, hoping it would give her the idea that the conversation was over. She didn't move.

"I've reported this to Deep-Three, and once they decide what to do with it, we can go from there," he said, walking toward the door. "At the least they'll give you the legal release paperwork so we can get the cargo back to its point of origin."

"That will involve penalties," she said, rising from the chair and turning to face him. "And I am going to have to file a report with CSL Shipping Control. You have a seriously injured crewman and that will require some accountability."

"For frak sake, he got overheated," he said.

"Dr. Caldwell says hyperthermia can be life threatening. She explained that it kills a lot of people on an annual basis on Starlight. Do not try to play this off as trivial, Captain. It isn't," she said, lowering her voice and squaring her shoulders. He could tell she was expecting to fight him over this.

"That may be true, but right now it doesn't matter what you do," he said, opening the door and nodding out toward the corridor. She still didn't move. "We are required by law to remain here until authorities release us."

"That only applies to a site of criminal activity. Nothing says this is a crime, and even if it is, then most certainly remaining here jeopardizes the security of the ship, the cargo and the crew," she said. "I am ready to cancel the contracts so we can return to Zone One now. Dr. Caldwell and Mr. Pruitt can make other arrangements after we return them to safety."

"They're not going to sit still for that," he said, almost laughing at her preposterous suggestion.

"It doesn't matter if they sit still or dance a jig." She stepped up close enough he could feel her breath on his face. "If I cancel the contract, you will be obligated to return the ship and its cargo to Zone One immediately."

"You can do that, but I will not break the law to protect company policy, or your precious contract. Without a release from the authorities, we're going nowhere. I've contacted FleetCom and as soon as we know what they want us to do, we can be on our way," he said. "So why don't you take a deep breath and get off my ass while we wait? I've got a ship to run and you have paperwork to file or something."

He pointed through the door and nodded. "We're done."

"You've got a problem with your attitude, Captain," she said as she stepped past him into the hall. "That will go in my report."

He shoved the door closed behind her and sighed. "And I don't think I care."

It would be a minimum of six days for her report to get to Zone One. If he got a comm back from Deep-Three, he'd have an answer, and probably the release, before her message got to headquarters.

CHAPTER SIX

WHEN CAPTAIN WALKER calmed down enough to decide it was time to eat, the only ones left on the mid-deck were his two passengers and Angelique Wolfe who sat at a discreet distance but maintained a watchful eye. Marti had told him that he'd find Kaycee and Elias waiting for him, so he snatched a bottle of his special reserve rum and three glasses from his liquor cabinet and headed down to tell them the situation.

He didn't like the situation, and he knew they'd like it less. His only hope was the alcohol would help what he had to tell them go down easier.

"How's Preston?" he asked, walking up and startling them both. He set the glasses on the table and poured them full before he sat down.

"He'll be fine," Kaycee said, picking her glass up and waiting until they'd all raised their glasses before she slammed it back like a veteran. "Once somebody gets overheated like that, it tends to make them more susceptible to future occurrences, but he's young so he'll bounce back."

"That's good news," Walker said, pouring another round and setting the bottle down on the opposite side of the table.

"I'd recommend getting good environmentally appropriate

gear before the next time he goes down," she said.

"Unfortunately, there isn't going to be a next time," he said, throwing the boulder on the table right up front.

"Excuse me?" Elias asked, downing his second shot and setting his glass back on the table. "You mean no next time for him, yes?"

He shook his head. "Not for any of us. At least not until we hear back from FleetCom."

"I expected you'd have to bring FleetCom into this," Kaycee said. Ethan caught the significant and obviously instructional glare she shot at Pruitt. "How long will it take to get permission to investigate?"

"I reported the situation to authorities at Cygnus Deep-Three and asked them what they want us to do. It's almost a fourteen-hour transmission lag each way, so the earliest we will hear back is sometime tomorrow secondshift," he said. "Until we receive an answer, we need to sit tight."

"A lot could happen in twenty-eight hours," Pruitt said.

"A lot has already happened down there," Walker said. "Whatever occurred, it was probably weeks ago. Another half day won't make much difference. I know that's not what you want to hear but until FleetCom weighs in—"

"My family is down there," Elias said, his eyes flashing. "I need to get to them, and this isn't something I care to debate with you, Captain."

"I understand that," he said. "Well, honestly, maybe I don't since I don't have a family other than my crew. But I do know how hard it must be."

"I don't think you do Ethan," Kaycee said, sounding like she was struggling to hold her own anger below the surface. "There are a hundred thousand colonists in Starlight. All of my brothers and sisters live there. My mother. My husband and my wife too."

Clouds drifted across her face and she looked down at the table.

"I know," he said, looking down too. "I can't do anything about it right now. I'm trying, but I just can't."

"Why not?" Elias growled. "This is your ship."

"Only on paper," the captain said. "I got my butt rather unceremoniously handed to me by my Triple-C. She made sure I understand I'm on dangerous ground."

"We have to do something. People could be dying while we sit up here and do nothing," Pruitt said. He grabbed the bottle, poured another dose of rum into his glass, and slammed the bottle down on the table with a solid thump.

"I don't think so," Walker said, shaking his head.

"What makes you say that?" he hissed as he bottomed his third drink in as many minutes.

Maybe it wasn't such a good idea to bring booze, he thought as he noticed Angel get up and move to a better position to keep an eye on them. As usual, the handler was in front of the potential problem.

Ethan let out a long slow sigh. "Not to put too a fine a point on it, but it's an oven down there. If there were massive collections of corpses, I'd have known it. By now they'd be stinking."

Pruitt slowly swung his eyes in the captain's direction and his face ran through a dozen expressions before it dissolved into a wall of pain.

"You can sit there and tell me you aren't going to find out what's going on?" Kaycee asked, acid edging into her tone.

"I can do exactly that," he said. "I have to tread very lightly or—"

"Very lightly be damned, Ethan," she snapped. "You cannot let her push you into ignoring your responsibilities."

"My responsibility is to this ship, and the passengers and cargo it carries," he said. "Solving this mystery is not on the list of things I can bite into."

"My entire life is down there. If you won't investigate, then let me."

"I can't," he said.

"You have to," she said.

He shook his head. "Seriously, Kaycee. From a legal standpoint you two are cargo. You contracted with Cochrane Space Logistics to carry you here. Until there's a safe place to deliver you and Elias, I cannot sign you over. The company has the responsibility to protect you."

"That's pure crap," Elias snarled.

"Actually, it's not," he said. "I can't do anything about it."

"It's not that you can't. You won't," Kaycee said.

"Leigh is the Cargo Compliance Controller. Do you know what that means?" he asked.

"Yah, she makes sure the cargo gets to where it is going," she said.

"It's more than that. She's responsible for the cargo," he said. "She's the legal agent for CSL. She works for them and represents their authority out here where laws might otherwise be thinly interpreted."

"So what?" Elias said.

"As a Triple-C, she has the final say in everything except ship operations," Walker said. "If she thinks I'm risking a payload, she has the right and power to jerk my Shipmaster license and void my lease on the *Olympus Dawn*. She can order my first officer to pilot the vessel back to Zone One. In that situation, if any of my crew refuses her orders, she can go as far as locking me down and calling in a replacement captain to get the ship home."

"So, she's got your bag in a vice," Kaycee said. "But I have the right to tell her to stuff it."

"Sure. You can request arbitration, but she has the authority to have you arrested for your own protection. Especially if she thinks you've become a risk to the cargo," he said.

"What?" Pruitt almost roared.

The captain nodded. "Protecting the cargo is her singular responsibility. That means she's obligated to protect you too. If your behavior endangers yourself, or the other cargo, she can have you confined until we make a port where arbitration services are available." He held up his hand to stop another explosion. "Go ahead and look it up. It is in the contract you signed before you came aboard."

"You're telling me that in her mind, going down to Starlight is a risk to me, and therefore the cargo," Kaycee said.

"Yes, exactly," he said. "Right now, she's probably in her office writing up a formal reprimand against me because she thinks I've already risked your safety. She told me she will be transmitting a report to CSL headquarters outlining how she feels I've already jeopardized you both."

"Howso?" she asked.

"Let's assume for the sake of argument that there's a virus loose on Starlight and that it's killed everything," he said. "If that's true, then I've taken a huge chance by going to the surface."

"But you did a medscan on the excursion party before you came back," she said, pausing in mid-thought and shaking her head as concern flashed over her face. "You did do that, didn't you?"

"Absolutely," he confirmed. "I'm really not a dumb as I look."

"It's possible that a new infectious organism might have popped up that the bioscan equipment wouldn't detect. If it is a virus, that means it got past the assessment survey of the planet." Elias said, picking up the bottle to pour himself another drink. Kaycee shot him a look that caused him to put it back on the table sheepishly.

"What Leigh said is true. If that happened, and we brought it back, then I'd be responsible."

"The odds of that are small," she said.

"I know that," Ethan said. "However, I have to admit that the chance of something like that is not zero. We have the best bio scanning gear we can get on a shuttle, but it's limited. There's only so much we can scan for."

"Your MedBay has high-end automation but is nowhere near well enough set up to catch everything," Elias said.

"Because we can't guarantee the environment on the surface is safe with the tools we've got, any more trips down there are a hard nogo."

"Theoretically speaking, if there wasn't a risk of exposure, would she authorize another excursion party?" Kaycee asked.

"Probably not," he said, shrugging. "That might take one of her arguments out from under her, but she's a certified legal advisor. Debating is her profession, and she'd just come up with a new position to counterattack. Arguing with her is like hugging a cactus."

"Ouch," Pruitt said, grinning in spite of his frustration.

"It doesn't matter, because we can't do the science to make sure it's safe with what we have onboard," the captain said.

Kaycee leaned back in her chair and crossed her arms. She glanced at Elias and he nodded slightly. "I could guarantee the environment from a biological perspective. We've got better gear in the payload."

"I figured you knew what we were carrying, even if you aren't listed as a load steward on the manifest. You know you're obligated to disclose that in the paperwork?" Ethan said, frowning. "But it doesn't matter. It's sealed until it's delivered, and she'd have to vacate the contract in order to let us crack the seals."

"You don't think she'd allow that, even in an emergency?"

he asked.

He shook his head. "In her world there are no emergencies, only bad planning. Her position would be that there's no proof of a problem, and without that, the load is sacrosanct."

"While people might be dying?" Elias said. His voice carried more anguish than anger this time as he gave voice to his fear again. He was clearly shredding inside.

"From her chair there's no evidence to suggest that as a real possibility," Ethan said. "Let's hope she's right."

Kaycee nodded, "And we can't get evidence without going down there."

"Exactly," the captain said. "And she won't let us open the load to prove it is safe to go down there, so we can't get the evidence. Law lives off of the art of circular logic."

"Nojo?" Elias asked. "She could be that callous to the potential reality?"

Ethan leaned back and sighed. "It's not callousness. She works by rules. Order comes from enforcing the law, and she believes that the structure that comes from that is the ultimate foundation of civilization, and likely the entire universe."

"And you can work with this woman?" Kaycee asked, shaking her head.

"Normally, she is just an over-qualified shipping clerk," he said. "In the three plus years I've had her as my watchdog, this is the first time we've gridlocked."

"So, to get her to change heading on this, we've got to tackle her arguments one by one," she said.

"You can try, but I don't think you're going to accomplish much," Walker said. "If you push hard enough, you might get her to agree to arbitration. But that means you don't have your say until we get to a facility where those legal services are available. Until then, as far as she's concerned, she is the incontrovertible representative and interpreter of law."

"My family is down there," Elias repeated as his face let loose and showed the torment he felt.

"Mine too," Kaycee said, swallowing hard and looking away. "Ethan, if you were in our place, what would you do?"

"Don't put me in that position," he said, standing up and slamming the last half of his second drink. "My whole life is this ship, and everyone that's on it is my family. You are asking me to throw my family away for the sake of finding out about yours. If I knew for sure that there was a real possibility that it would make a difference, I'd probably risk it, but…" he shook his head, leaving the rest of the thought unsaid.

He stepped back a half pace and closed his eyes for a second. "I'm sorry, but I've already gotten myself in way deep over this. I know how frustrating it is for you, but she's got my hands tied. Leigh made sure I understood precisely how precarious my position is."

CHAPTER SEVEN

"Boss you need to report to MedBay now."

Ethan woke from a restless night of kicking and thrashing his way through near nightmares. He wasn't sure he'd actually heard Rene's voice, or if it had been in a dream.

He rolled over and glanced at the chrono on his bedside shelf. Its faint illumination told him it was 0400.

"What's up?" he asked, tentatively. If the voice had been real, he'd get a reply, and if not, then maybe he could go back to sleep.

"You need to get down here now," he said, this time the urgency was clear in Rene's voice.

"Is it Preston?" he asked, fear grabbing at his heart with a steel claw. Kaycee had told him he was recovering. Maybe he'd relapsed somehow?

"For the third time, Boss. You need to get down here quick. Before any of the rest of the crew gets here."

"Is Preston alright?" he snarled. "Just tell me that."

"Yah, he's fine, but we've got a big problem and you need to get on top of this now," Rene said.

"Fine I'm on my way," he said, pushing the coverlet off and tapping the screen on his console to bring up the lights.

It took less than three minutes to get dressed and down to

the mid-deck, but when he skidded to a stop at the MedBay door, he wasn't sure he was awake enough to understand what he was looking at. It looked like a pasta processor had come apart all over everything, with chunks of unrecognizable hardware strung together with ropes of opti-cables and power lines. It was a hideous mess and, for all that he tried to absorb the reality of what he was seeing, he had no clue what was going on.

"What the hell is all this?" he asked. His guts told him that he didn't want to know.

"My gear," Kaycee said, stepping out from behind a console. She wore a lab smock and had an optical visor over her face and had an augment arm strapped over her shoulder.

"Your gear?" he asked. "From the cargo module?"

"Yah. It's a small part of it," she said, flipping the faceplate up and smiling at him like she was oblivious of the consequences of what she'd done.

"You got Leigh to unlock the seal for you?"

"Uhm … Not exactly." Her smile wrinkled on the side and he would have laughed except he knew were this was going. *His guts were right.*

"Then, how'd you get it?" He drew in a breath and held it while he waited for the answer he knew was coming.

Elias stood up from behind another piece of equipment and waved sheepishly.

"What the holy frak?" he bellowed. "You can't just unseal the cargo without getting her to write it off! Oh shit, no!"

"We need to do a deeper scan on the three of you to prove it's not dangerous down there," Kaycee said. "After our discussion last night, I realized I had to address her concerns over the risk. I had to have access to my equipment to do that."

Ethan dropped back against the wall and thumped his head against it repeatedly.

"You have … you can't …" he sputtered.

"Just breathe," she said. Her eyes showed her confusion. "I'll take responsibility for it."

"You cannot do that," he said. "As captain I have the sole responsibility for everything that happens aboard the ship. You cannot take that off of me."

"I'll talk to her," she said. "She'll understand we needed to do this to prove you didn't put us in danger."

"This could end my command."

"Oh, you're being melodramatic," she said.

"The frag I am," he growled, anger overtaking his other emotions in a wave. "You have no clue how serious this is. Cargo tampering is a criminal offense."

"But it's my cargo—"

"It belongs to Smythe Biomedical, but it doesn't matter." He launched away from the wall with both elbows. He needed to figure out his options and somehow explain the reality to her. "I have custodial responsibility for everything in that payload container until we unload it at port. If it doesn't arrive at its destination in an uncompromised state … meaning exactly the same condition that it left the shipper, they can prosecute me under the internal piracy laws."

"That sounds draconian," Elias said.

"I am sure it won't come to that," she added, nodding.

"It seriously might," Rene said, jumping to the captain's defense. "It used to be fairly common for ships to arrive at their destinations a little light in the load. A lot of crews were making more cred by skimming off cargo and then selling what they'd boosted on the underground market. It got bad enough that the government imposed laws to protect shippers from bad crews and to cut back on illegal markets. They don't frak around with it."

"Well, I'm sorry, but there's nothing we can do about it now,"

Kaycee said. "I have no intention of putting it back. If we're going to do anything about what's going on down on Starlight, we need to rule out any pathogens first."

He shook his head and spun to walk away. It was either that or risk damaging the passenger part of his cargo in a very real way.

"I'll need to do an exam on you once I get this all set up," she said.

Walker didn't slow down on the way out.

He headed across the lounge toward the galley and a cup of pseudojo. It was still several hours before his usual morning, but the instant coffee-like oil, would at least give him something else to grumble about while he stewed over the ever deepening pit opening under him.

He sat down on a stool in front of the VAT dispenser and watched as his thermocup filled. "Marti how did they get into the cargo module without tripping the alarm?"

"That is a good question, Captain," it said.

"Why the hell didn't you see them hauling things out of there?"

"My systems seem to be functioning normally," Marti said. "I have no record of either of them being in the cargo interconnect corridor."

"You've got optics in there. Were they working?"

"Yes. I have a continuous record from those areas," it said.

"They had to have shut them down somehow," he said as he took his cup and walked back out to a table. He would have taken a chair, but he needed to pace so only sat his cup down. "Wouldn't that have pinged you?"

"The first visual record I have of the incident is after they transported their hardware to the MedBay."

"It didn't just appear there," he said.

"Agreed. It would be possible to spoof the broadcast system

that carries the optic data, but I do not detect any evidence of a point where they interrupted the signal."

"Is it possible that they didn't do that? Could they have accessed your memory files directly and deleted the records?"

"That is extremely unlikely," it said, almost managing to sound indignant at the implication. "However, as I anticipated this question, I have conducted a complete diagnostic of my logic system. I am unaltered."

"If you have no record of them breaking into the payload, and we know they've done it, then one of those two possibilities has to have happened," he said.

"Undeniably, this is true," Marti said. "I am working to find where the breach occurred."

"Where were the handlers while this was going on?" he asked. "Nuko had posted them to guard Pruitt at least."

"In their quarters. Crewman Wolfe had just completed a double shift and Crewman Chandler was sleeping. We determined that I would monitor the corridor outside Mr. Pruitt's stateroom and alert them if he left for any reason. They had both been on duty for eighteen hours out of the last day-cycle when the passengers retired for the night."

"So, it wasn't just the cargo interconnect that they spoofed, it was the passenger deck, too.

"Yes, Captain," Marti said.

"I am just going to take a guess here. You also didn't see them setting up their gear in the MedBay either?"

"I was unaware of their activity until Engineer Pascalle alerted me."

"How does that happen?" he asked. "Were you asleep?"

"I do not sleep," it said. "However, discovering that I apparently have holes in my perception is a decidedly unsettling realization."

Humans have them, too," Rene said, walking up and joining the conversation. "We get used to them."

"I am aware of this concept, although holes in my perception could adversely affect the safety of the ship," the AA said. "Because of this, I am continuing my diagnostic self-examination at a circuitry level."

"Good, if you hadn't said that, I'd have ordered it," Walker said. He stopped pacing and circled back to his cup. "Who is watching them?"

"Billiam just hit the deck," he said, leaning forward to look down into the captain's cup. He wrinkled his nose and stood back up. "Damn, is the VAT broke again?"

He shrugged and winced as he picked it up and took a swallow.

"I told him to keep them on eyeball lock until you made a decision on what to do," Rene said as he took the cup and set it down on a different table. Downwind.

"Excuse me, Captain, we need a power hookup in the MedBay," Kaycee said from across the deck. "Is there any chance you can get Rene to drop us a cable from somewhere?"

"No." He shook his head and looked at his engineer to make sure he understood that was an order. "Absolutely, no way."

"Without it we can't get the nuclear-imaging multiplexer working," she said, coming across the room, apparently with the idea that she could negotiate.

"I don't care, I said no," he said. "You commit a crime that you're going to get me buried for, and then you want me to compound it by helping you?"

"You're being unreasonable Ethan," she said. Her smile only fed into his determination.

"Unreasonable?" he hissed. "Do you even have a clue what you've done? I should lock you up and pray that they vent your ass for it and don't blame me."

"She's right, Boss, maybe you are overreacting a bit here," Rene said. "The damage is already done, and the only way you're going to come out of this on the other end is to let it play out and hope she can swing enough water to justify it."

"Are you serious?" he asked, shooting a skeptical eye at the engineer.

He nodded. "I think we've got no choice but to go all in and hope for the best. If they can prove it's safe on the surface, then maybe, if FleetCom arrives before Leigh has a complete apoplectic seizure, they might be able to mitigate things on your behalf."

"A word please … alone." The captain turned his back on Kaycee and walked across the room, pulling Rene along by his arm. When they were far enough away not to be overheard, he lowered his voice and shook his head. "You do realize that if I say yes, and let you get them hooked up, it moves you from simply being a witness to a crime, to being a full-on accomplice. Right now, you've not crossed any lines, and I might have a chance to argue for leniency when they bring me up on charges. But if we go along at all, we're both going to be in the shit over it. You for doing it, and me for letting you."

Rene stared off over Ethan's shoulder for several seconds as he chewed over what that might mean. Finally, he nodded. "I've served with you now since you leased the *Olympus Dawn*. You've been one of the best captains I've ever had, and I hope to work with you a lot longer. The problem is that if you don't let her prove that you've not jeopardized the cargo, then you're going down for it. That's what will end your career."

"It's probably over even if she does," Walker said. "At the very least CSL will jerk my lease and I'll lose the ship."

"That might happen," he said, nodding. "I'm willing to face

taking the shot with you, if it will help them pull the skunk out of the bathtub."

"That's a big jump into some damned stinking water," the captain said.

"I know, but we've got to stick together in this. If we don't, what's the point?"

"Here's the problem," he said. "What good does it do if she proves that we're clean of contamination? You know she's only doing it to justify going back down there. I can't let that happen."

"Fine. You and I both know that," Rene said, "but it keeps the two of them working and distracted until FleetCom gives you an answer. That shouldn't be too much longer, yes?"

He nodded. "Another fifteen hours or so."

"And they will at the least be sending a ship to investigate?"

Again, Walker nodded. "Probably, but I don't know."

"Then the more she can figure out before their reply gets here, the easier you make the job for them," he said. "That has to be worth something."

"That's not going to be enough to justify violating a transportation contract," the captain said. "FleetCom's not willing to take a position that goes against a Triple-C, most of the time."

"Maybe not, but who knows? FleetCom does operate on a different set of priorities, and it certainly can't hurt to have a ten-ton elephant who owes you a favor," Rene said. "In the end, it'll all depend on what's really happening on Starlight."

Ethan glanced back over his shoulder at Kaycee. She was staring at him with her arms crossed and drumming her fingers on her bicep impatiently. "Frag it all to frakking hell," he whispered.

"I'm willing to risk it," Rene said. "We've always been in this together, and if I get messy trying to pull your ass out of the fire, then I think I can at least live with the fact that I did it for the right reasons."

Closing his eyes, the captain nodded. "Do it."

He turned around and stared at the doctor for a minute. "Before you get back to work Doctor, I need a word with you."

"Of course," she said, pitching her head to send Rene toward where Elias stood watching from a distance.

"I want you to understand one thing," he said, sitting down at the nearest table and waiting for her to join him. "You have just ended my career, and probably that of my engineer."

"I will do my best to put in a mitigating word for you both," she said. "I'm sorry that this might land you in trouble. That wasn't my intent."

"Probably not, but there's no doubt that you've done it anyway," he said. "I just want one concession from you."

"As long as it doesn't mean I can't do my work," she said.

"If you don't want to be spending the rest of the time you're aboard the *Olympus Dawn* locked up, you do not do another end run around me. Do I make myself perfectly clear?"

"Yes, Captain," she said. Her eyes said she meant it sincerely, but he doubted he could trust her.

"I hope I can figure out how to keep my Triple-C from demanding I escort you through an airlock and then follow you out," he said. "I'll try to buy you time so that you can figure out what you need to know, but like I said last night, she does have the authority to relieve me of command and order your arrest."

"Do you think she'll do that?" she asked, looking like she might be finally starting to take him seriously about what Leigh could do.

"I cannot guarantee what she'll do when she comes down pissed," he said. "Any possibility is on the deck at this point."

"I get that—"

She stopped abruptly as the Triple-C appeared out of the lift.

Chaos exploded in the next instant.

"Now you can see what I mean," the captain said as he stood up and turned to face the Valkyrie queen.

CHAPTER EIGHT

"Is the ship mine now?" Nuko asked as Ethan came through the door onto the ConDeck and threw himself into the seat behind his console.

He shot her a face full of frustration heavy enough that she flinched.

"Oops, sorry," she said.

He let out a long slow breath and shook his head. "You don't know how close you came to nailing that one hard."

"Nojo?" she asked.

"I've listened to her quoting legal scripture until my brain went flat," he said. "I'm really so far down the screw-hole right now and she made sure I know she's got the torque to put the twisty end right through me."

"Seriously, all this is over them breaking the seal on the load?"

He nodded. "In her mind it's not trivial at all. I've been fighting all afternoon to keep her from having you lock me up."

"I wouldn't do it," she said. Her eyes told him she meant it.

"Yes, you would, because I wouldn't let you throw your career away trying to defend me." He wanted to pace but forced himself to stay in his chair. "Rene's misguided sense of loyalty might have already done that to him, and I won't be responsible for taking you both down with me."

"What? How?" she asked, turning her seat to face him.

"He helped Kaycee and Elias get their stuff hooked up," he said. "Legally, it makes him an accomplice after the fact."

"Accomplice?" She frowned as she tried to make that fit into her understanding. As a cargo pilot with a Shipmaster 4 license, she didn't have the same training that his Shipmaster certification required, so it didn't make sense to her. "Is she really this bent, because the doctor cracked her own cargo open?"

"Yah. The truth is that the cargo is owned by Smythe Biomedical. I don't know if Kaycee is a shareholder in the company, but even if she was, she doesn't have the right to access the content," he said. "It's probably a civil matter on whether they choose to prosecute her for attempted piracy, but since they didn't list her as the Cargo Steward on the manifest, she didn't have the right to open it up. Once a payload is loaded to a ship, other than with a warrant, the only persons who can open it are the Triple-C and the Cargo Steward."

"Right, I handle that end of the paperwork all the time when I'm loading," she said. "The steward is the representative of the cargo itself."

"Exactly," he said, nodding. "The problem is, they didn't want to list Kaycee on the manifest in case we were boarded."

"There's something that valuable in the load?"

"I don't know. I just drive," he said. "But Leigh told me they chose to leave it sealed, so there is no connection between the payload and the passengers."

"Does she plan on locking them up too?" Nuko asked.

"So far, no. I spent the last seven hours letting her scream at me, so she vented enough pressure not to explode and make a bad situation worse," he said. "By the end of it I managed to get her to agree to wait until FleetCom responds. It's fortunate for me that we're hanging in a situation that is squarely between the internal piracy laws, and the civil laws. After much shouting, she saw the wisdom in waiting for one system to make a decision, before she brings the other one into it."

"That's a skinny wall to be hiding behind," she said, frowning and glaring at the back of her hands.

He nodded. "She's filing a formal report, but she agreed that she won't implement anything until after we hear back."

"If she's filing another report, that will sit stinky with CSL."

"Actually, she held off on the first one," he said. "She knew I was trying to do the right thing, even if she thinks I frakked it up. She was planning to wait, and that's how I got her to hold off on taking action on this one for the time being."

"That's probably a plus."

"Yah maybe, but I'm thinking it'll just make it bite harder when she packs it all up in a big open reprimand." He shrugged. "It could be the beginning of the end, anyway. It probably is for me."

They sat in silence as they both stared out the window at an electrical storm exploding over Starlight's northern polar region. It arced and danced in slow rolling waves of lightning and he couldn't help thinking it looked like his life felt, at the moment. Flashing. Angry. Rapidly becoming dangerous, and out of control.

Nuko got up and stretched. "What is it they unpacked? Looked like a snake ball in the MedBay when I was getting firstmeal this morning."

"It still does," he said. "Biomedical gear mostly. Some of it I recognize, but some of it is totally beyond me. She's done scans on the three of us that went down, and on Angel and Billy."

"Why's she scanning them?"

"Something about a baseline calibration," he said. "She

wouldn't say what it was she was looking for, just that when it finished, she'd have a complete assessment of any foreign crud we might have picked up, regardless of any crud being recognizable or not."

"That's got to be a pretty thorough test then," she said.

He nodded. "Probably, but it only took a few minutes."

"I know she's a doctor and all that, but has she explained why they're bringing all this fancy med-gear to the ass end of humanity?"

"I asked her about that while she was scanning me, and all she'd say was that she was a research doctor of some kind, and it was specialty equipment that they needed for their hospital," he said. "Apparently, they're bringing in 500,000 new colonists for some mining project here and they need this gear to do the upgrades."

Nuko twisted her face into a caricature of skepticism.

"I only know what she told me," he said. "Stinks funny to me too, but with the shit storm today it's hard to tell one bad smell from another."

"Nuko Takata, please report to my office," Leigh Salazar said over the open comm.

"I'm on the ConDeck. Let me lock down my station and I'll be right there," she said, shaking her head. "She knew where I was. She didn't need to broadcast that on ship wide."

"She's probably making sure we all know she's going through the formal process," he said. "I expected she'd want to talk to you sooner or later. It just means she hasn't finished her report. Or that she's changed her mind about holding off and is going to have you take me out of the chair."

"That is a correct assessment, Captain," Marti said.

"Which?" Nuko asked as she leaned over her seat and logged out of her console.

66

"She has not accessed the deep-comm system at this point, and I can therefore assume she has not completed her report."

"Damn it. I don't want to do this," she said.

"If she hasn't finished, odds are she's not going to order you to relieve me," Walker said. "If she decides to do that, she'll wait until she has her paperwork in place and do it by the book. Hopefully, that will take her a while."

"I can't believe she'll ruin your career because you went down to the surface once," she said. "It seems like such a trivial thing."

"She might have let the excursion go if that was all there was, but the problem with civilization is that it makes laws and then uses them to amplify the miniscule to the point of absurdity."

"It's still wrong," she said as her control console shut down.

"No it's not wrong, it's just hard," he said. "I did violate company policy and to some extent broke the law too. Regardless of how justified it seems, I didn't do what I should've done, because I thought it was right to do the wrong thing."

She wrinkled her face and stuck a finger in her ear and wiggled it like she was trying to shake his words around to make sense out of them.

"I know that sounded twisty, but you know what I mean." He winked at her. "I'll pay for this however it works out, and if I'm lucky, there might be enough mitigating circumstances to keep me from being in it too deep. If not, then it will run where it has to run."

"How the hell can you be so calm while she's trying to figure out how to ruin you?"

"She's really not," he said, shaking his head. "She's trying to figure out how to protect the cargo with the least amount of damage to all of us. It's what she does, and what she has to do."

"Still—"

"Just go and talk to her." He waved his hand toward the door.

"I'll hold the deck for as long as she lets me."

Once the door had closed behind her, he popped up from his seat and paced the small riser along the back of the ConDeck. It was too small to walk off his frustration but being in motion felt a little better than sitting and watching the storm gathering. He knew he had to keep his real level of irritation from visibly erupting, but it was tough, especially when he was trying to defend the person who wanted to end his career.

He had to keep peace on the ship, so he swallowed it and put on the mask. Fortunately, the conversation hadn't gone on longer or he might not have been able to keep his true rage bottled up.

"Captain you are receiving a transmission from the FleetCom Multicruiser *Magellan*," Marti said, interrupting his three hundredth orbit of the deck.

"Not from Deep-Three?" he asked.

"Negative," it said.

"Put it through," he said, dropping back into his chair and opening the comm. A woman's face appeared on the screen, behind her the control deck seemed to disappear into the distance. He'd never seen the *Magellan*, but it was one of the new Explorer Class multicruisers. The expanse of open space over her shoulder looked to be bigger than the entirety of his ship.

"FCM *Magellan* to CSV-1070 *Olympus Dawn*. You are instructed to remain on station at K-186e Starlight until we can rendezvous and complete a situational assessment. Continue monitoring for signs of life or communication signals. Should you detect either, you are to contact the *Magellan* directly before taking any action.

"Under no circumstances are you to return to the surface of Starlight.

"We will be over the threshold at K-186 in thirty-nine hours at 0940 hours Zone One Standard Time.

"Colleen MacKenna, Captain, *Magellan*. Out."

Walker sat for almost a minute before Marti asked, "Do you want to confirm receipt of the instructions?"

"Yah, sorry," he said. "I was thinking it sounded like there was something else that Captain MacKenna wasn't saying."

"Why do you say that?"

"I'm not sure. It felt like there was more that she could have said but didn't."

Marti paused for almost two whole seconds. "Human intuition is a delicate contrivance. Now that you are facing a personal crisis, is it possible, that you are coloring your interpretation of Captain MacKenna's message with an emotional desire to externalize the cause of your circumstance?"

"I think that's got to be the most polite way I have ever heard to call someone paranoid," he said, shrugging off the implication. "You're right though, I might be grasping at straws."

Swiveling in his chair, he tapped the control to bring the deep-comm transmitter up. When the green indicator flashed that the system was up he cleared his throat.

"CSV-1070 *Olympus Dawn* to FCM *Magellan*. Captain MacKenna Instructions received. Standing by. We will rendezvous with you on 2368.014. Be aware that there is no signal from the beacon, so navigation in the system is by local reckoning.

"Safe travels. Walker, Commander *Olympus Dawn*. Out."

He punched the icon to transmit the message, his mind hanging on the fact that this might be the last official message of his career.

Nuko was right, it seemed damned trivial to hang him for just doing a quick walkabout. *But that's not the only infraction*, he reminded himself once again.

He sighed. "That certainly puts a timeline on my command doesn't it?"

"Perhaps," Marti said. "It also means you will have to inform the passengers that regardless of the results of their analysis, they will not be allowed to go down to the planet."

"That's true, but at least they can't blame me for that. It's on FleetCom now."

CHAPTER NINE

ETHAN KNEW EVERYTHING around him was winding into an uncontrollable spin. No matter which of the dozen ways the situation might play out, he knew he had no choice but to keep pushing through and hope he could eventually steer it to the softest possible landing. The farther he tore into the details in his mind, the more convinced he was that CSL would, at the minimum, slap him with a fine and formal reprimand. If it went down hard, he could lose his lease on the *Olympus Dawn*.

Especially if Smythe or CSL pushed forward with charges of internal piracy.

Because he'd not been paying attention, he'd allowed his passengers to cross a line that he was responsible to hold. It was the biggest thing hanging over him. He should have anticipated that Kaycee would try to do something like this. He knew she was desperate to learn what had happened to the colony. He should have taken precautions to make sure neither of them could circumvent his orders. In that, he screwed up.

Doing an excursion to the surface before he alerted the authorities wasn't a minor thing, but whether that was endangering the crew and payload was still up for debate. If they hadn't brought anything contagious back to the ship from

Starlight, then luck might give him an edge in defending himself, when all the incident reports were filed.

When Nuko got back to her quarters after her interview, she gave him a bit of good news by letting him know the Triple-C wasn't trying to take him down. Leigh was trying to figure out how to avoid filing a formal report. Unfortunately, she told Nuko that she felt like there were no options. The Triple-C had come out and told her that she was shuffling things along as slowly as possible.

Depending on how things played once the *Magellan* arrived, there might be enough water swinging in the situation to get him off gentle. It still was far from inevitable that it would cost him his command, but he knew it was prudent to brace for the worst, even if he wanted to hope for the best.

Since the ship flew with no need for human supervision, he'd only stayed on the ConDeck to be out of reach to his passengers. The entire upper deck was off limits to all but the crew, and he used it to hide. There were only two passengers aboard, but since they were the biggest source of his frustration, he needed to be away from them to think.

He had a small ready room behind the ConDeck. It had a command console and a conference table with enough chairs to seat the entire crew as long as everyone had recently showered. He seldom used it, so it was a good place to sit alone with his thoughts.

He'd propped his feet up on the corner of the table and was reclining with his eyes closed and his fingers laced behind his head when Kaycee appeared at his door unannounced. "Captain, can I have a word with you?"

No, he thought, but he held his tongue. Her presence snapped him back to the immediate world. He didn't care at this point if he offended her or not, but she wasn't alone. Preston and

Rene both stood behind her looking apologetic. He needed to maintain appearances in front of his people.

She sat down without waiting for him to invite her in. *She's obviously used to pissing uphill,* he thought, frowning as he nodded to chairs at the other end of the table. Both men took the seats he'd indicated. "I assume you're here because you've got results?"

"Yah," she said, pulling a thinpad out of her coverall and sliding it across the table in his direction.

He didn't pick it up, but he glanced at the screen. "Since I don't speak doctor, what's it say?"

"I did a Genotype Replication Analysis on all three of you and then did a fractional-biographic-projection to compare your scans to the baseline I ran on Wolfe and Chandler. The results came back negative."

"Sure, whatever that means," he said. "I assume negative is a good thing?"

She nodded. "What that means is I built a mathematical model of each of you and compared the actual organic scans against the absolute replicate form to determine there were no alterations to the real you."

Walker wrinkled up his forehead and rubbed his fingers over the creases. He shook his head. "I still don't follow you." He pinned Preston with a glare and added, "Do you understand what she's saying here?"

"A little," he said, shrugging. "She's saying we're clean, but I am not sure how she got the answer."

"That's all I need to know, I guess," the captain said. "I think I'd hurt myself trying to chase you into the fascinating world of whatever this 'genotype replication' thing is."

"I did a deep genetic scan, and then cloned you, *mathematically.* This allowed me to reproduce your structure, plus all the microflora that normally lives inside your body."

"People are all basically communities of microscopic bacteria and other stuff living together inside our skin suit," Preston clarified.

"The replication I did, allowed me to model everything that's supposed to be inside you accurately," she said. "With that I could do a comparison of what was really there, versus the projection. Anything that showed up as not being indigenous in your metabolism, I flagged and chased to ground."

"As long as you're certain we've got nothing inside us we shouldn't have, then I can take that to Leigh and let her know her concerns about risk are unfounded," Walker said.

"I am one hundred percent sure of that," she said. "There was only one thing that was consistently abnormal in all of your scans. Fortunately, it wasn't something contagious."

"Is it a problem?" he asked, looking back down at the thinpad like he expected to understand more of it than he had before.

"Not at the level I detected, but it is concerning," she said. "You've all three picked up traces of an unusual radioactive residue in your lungs. It's well below the cumulative level for ionization so there's little risk at this low dose level."

"I assume it's from something we breathed in down there?" he asked.

"It looks like dust particles. Only the three of you show signs of it," she said. "The control scans I did on Wolfe and Chandler didn't detect any of the contamination.

"Dust covered everything down there. Is it indigenous to the local environment?"

"No. And that's what troubles me," she said. "Something has created a low-level background radiation that wasn't there before. We would have picked it up on the original assessment of the planet."

"Is it possible it was low enough level that it fell below the threshold of note?" Rene asked.

"If it was, you wouldn't have accumulated enough in your systems from a few hours of exposure to be detectable," she said. "Something with this high a level in the environment would have made the cumulative effect concerning for colonists living their entire life on Starlight."

"How long would a person have to be exposed to it to be dangerous?" the captain asked.

She shrugged. "Probably years. But it was enough that I picked it up on my conventional detecting gear and not on my special equipment."

"We need to talk about her gear for a minute," Rene said.

Why?" Ethan asked. Her equipment was a sore issue since it was still the big stink-storm hanging over him.

"When I volunteered to help them hook up their hardware, I realized something was way out of spec," he said. "They needed almost half our combined reactor output to run their stuff."

The captain whistled.

"If we'd been running in cruise, we couldn't have powered the field and the MedBay at the same time," Rene said.

"What kind of medical equipment takes that kind of power?" he asked, leaning forward and putting his elbows on the table.

"You're going to love this," the engineer said, nodding and grinning.

"I don't think so," Walker said.

"I've got some hardware from the Shan Takhu Institute in the payload modules," she said. "STI gave me a research loan—"

"Shan Takhu technology? I didn't think they'd released any of the alien tech into the wild," he said.

"Your ship is loaded with it," she said. "Where do you think you got artificial gravity and faster than light engines?"

"That's different. We built it ourselves by reverse engineering their designs," he said. "I assume that is why we picked up the load at Armstrong Station?"

"I studied at the STI Biosciences Research University on L-4 Prime," she said. "I worked under Professor Drake for five years before they credentialed me to do my own work."

"Dr. Tana Drake? Holy frak she's like the mother of all non-terrestrial medicine," Preston said, his eyes going wide in a severe case of rapid-onset hero worship.

She nodded and winked at the med-tech. "I wrote a research proposal in my last year of post-doc studies there and she offered me a chair in one of their departments. When I got called home, they almost canceled the project, but Smythe Biomedical picked it up and leveraged STI to loan out some of their cool toys."

"We're carrying alien technology, and nobody thought to tell me that?" the captain asked.

"I'm sorry, but they decided to keep it down low because of the security risk," she said, looking embarrassed and frustrated enough for both of them. "The less that people know, the less the odds of it catching the attention of undesirables."

"I assume Leigh knows?" he asked.

"That would explain why she's against the ceiling so hard," Rene said. "That's stuff that would be irreplaceable if anything happened to it."

She shrugged. "I haven't discussed it with her, but I'm sure the descriptions of the hardware on the manifest are pretty technical, so she might not understand exactly what it is. Although if she did any homework, she could have figured it out."

"Pruitt is your private security for this?" the captain asked.

"No, he's really a bio-med systems engineer," she said. "At least as far as I was told. He's from Starlight, and Smythe hired him to install the equipment when we got home. He happened to be visiting Earth after doing an internship at STI."

Walker glanced at Rene, who shot him a skeptical eye. Obviously, they were both on the same screen when it came to Elias.

"Well the good news is you've proved that we're not all about to die of Starlight Fever or whatever," the captain said. "I'll go tell Leigh. That will make at least one of my black marks a bit grayer."

"It's a start," the engineer said.

Ethan pushed back from the table and stood. "Thank you, Doctor—"

"There's one more thing I need to discuss with you," she said.

Here it comes, he thought crashing back into his chair. "Unfortunately, the answer is no," he said, anticipating her question.

She blinked in surprise and opened her mouth to protest, but he cut her off.

"Before you start arguing with me, I got an answer from FleetCom and they said that under no circumstances are we to go down to the surface unless we detect signs of life or get a signal. And then, only with permission."

"Why not?" she asked, anger and frustration showing in equal measure on her face.

"They didn't say, but you can take it up with Captain MacKenna when the *Magellan* arrives," he glanced at the chrono over the door. "They should be here in about thirty-four hours."

"But at the least we need to get a sample of the soil to see if we can confirm it contains the same radioactive signature that's in your lungs," she said.

"It's out of my hands," he said, shaking his head and making sure she understood that it was non-negotiable. "I understand how you feel, but for now you can stay busy by getting your equipment packed back into the cargo modules."

"We might need it again," she said.

"No, we won't," he said. "The *Olympus Dawn* isn't a science vessel, and I'm not going to have your toys lying around and reminding my Triple-C how far out of spec this has all gotten. Pack it up and put it away."

"Ethan, please ..." she said, stopping herself when he stood up again and she realized he was done with the discussion.

Leaning forward he put both his hands on the table in front of him. "Doctor, I understand that you are used to being a person of some importance in your field, but I don't care who you are in that world," he said. "You don't realize how close you've come to ending my career or perhaps you simply don't care. In either case, I'm done with it. You are on my ship, and you will do what I say, or I will have my people do it for you. If you force me to do that, I will have you confined to your quarters until I can hand you over to the *Magellan*. Is that clear enough?"

She sat motionless for several seconds before she nodded.

CHAPTER TEN

ETHAN SAT AT A DINING TABLE on the mid-deck watching Preston and Rene supervising Elias and Kaycee. The two of them were breaking things down and packing them away. They'd started at 0600 according to Marti, and his two cargo handlers had been keeping an eye on the process since they'd first set foot on the deck. He had stationed one outside MedBay and the other was watching the interconnect tube that allowed access to the payload modules.

He'd given orders that when they had safely stowed their equipment, they were to retract the connecting corridor and power down the containers. It wasn't standard procedure to cut off the support connections, but he wanted to make it as difficult as possible for his passengers to decide they needed to get back in to pull something else out.

It had taken them almost twelve hours to hook it all up and from the rate of progress, he expected it to take at least that long to get it all returned to the cargo container. He expected to have to sit guard duty for at least part of the shift, but he refused to let them work unsupervised at any point.

Leigh emerged from the galley carrying a cup of pseudojo and a tray with her breakfast and made her way across the room toward the lift cage. From her body language, she knew she had lost several points in popularity amongst the crew. She was right, but Ethan also knew he had to swallow his feelings and make peace with her, if this was ever going to work out in any way other than a disaster.

Waving, he called to her and then waited for her to realize it was an invitation to join him. She made her way over and stood there holding her food until he gestured toward the seat across from him. "Please. Join me," he said.

She cocked her head to the side but sat her tray on the table and lowered herself into the chair.

"I want you to understand that I know you are just doing your job," he said. "It's your ass on the line if you don't do it."

She nodded.

"Nuko told me that you were trying to figure out how to keep this from blowing all kinds of sidewise. And for that I thank you."

"Ethan," she started, pushing herself back into her seat with the edge of the table. She locked her elbows in place as she chewed over her words. Finally, she let out a sharp breath. "I don't want to ruin you. Honestly, you are one of the better captains with CSL, and I do like you."

"I try," he said, picking up his own coffee and grimacing as he took a sip. Rene still hadn't fixed the VAT.

Relaxing a bit, she flipped the lid off her breakfast and poked at it with a fork. "Most Triple-Cs are lucky to hold a posting for eighteen months, but you've run a spotless operation for the three years I've been with you. I know that's not an easy thing to do, and it's why I've been aboard this long. It's also why I'm so surprised that this situation has gotten so far out of spec."

He nodded, glancing over to where Elias was heaving one of the bigger pieces of gear onto a worksled. Rene was watching and being careful not to even get within an arm's reach of the equipment after he'd been told not to touch anything where Leigh might see it.

"I'm trying to clean up the mess if I can," he said.

"I understand from talking to Rene that you don't know how they got access in the first place," she said.

He nodded. "Somehow, Elias was able to circumvent the optics in several portions of the ship. Short of tying him to a chair and beating him with a stick, we don't have any way of knowing how he did it."

Her eyes got big at the mere suggestion of it and he laughed. "I was kidding. For the most part."

She wobbled her head in a vague circle like she was trying to figure out if he was serious or having a go with her. "I want to state categorically that torturing a passenger definitely counts as damaging cargo. And a bunch of other laws and stuff we don't even want to imagine. Even talking about it might be against company policy."

He snapped his fingers and winked at her. "That's no fun."

"Together Marti and Rene can't figure out what he did?"

"Not a clue," he said. "There are only two ways he could have done it, and neither of them is likely to be within the realm of possibility."

"So, what's to stop them from breaking back into the cargo if they want?"

"Once they're done packing it out, we're pulling the interconnect and powering the containers down," he said. "Once that's done Rene will disconnect the power to the tube and lock the breakers out. Without a cutting torch he won't be able to re-extend the corridor and the only way in then will be in an EVA suit or with this." He pulled a small silver disk from his pocket and tapped the side. A jagged edged flange popped out.

"That looks like an antique lockset piece," she said, picking it up to examine it.

"I had Rene fabricate the locks and the key last night after I ordered them to put their crap away," he said.

She handed the key back, but he shook his head. "You keep it. We don't need it to lock the breakers down and then once that's done, you're the only one in the universe that can extend the interconnect back."

"Without a cutting torch," she added.

"And using a torch in engineering would set off every environmental alarm on the ship," he said. "It's not foolproof, but it will slow them down enough that we can get in there and stop them before they sin again."

"How long do you think it will be before you lock it down?" she asked, dropping the key into the front of her thinskin and letting it settle to an intimate position where no one would consider chasing it.

"They'll have everything put back in the cargo modules by late this evening," he said. "Long before the *Magellan* gets here."

"The *Magellan*? That's a multicruiser isn't it?" she asked. "Why are they sending so much muscle this far out?"

"Yah, it is," he confirmed, surprised she'd know the name of a FleetCom naval vessel. "Unless something happens, it'll drop into the system tomorrow morning and rendezvous with us by late firstshift. As to why, it might have just been the nearest asset they had in the Cygnus Sector, but I can only guess what it was doing clear out here."

"Did they tell you what they wanted you to do?" She picked up her drink and sniffing it, blinked several times before she decided to pass.

"They ordered us to stay put and not return to the surface under any circumstances. They want us to monitor for signals or life signs."

"If we detect any, then what?" she asked.

"Captain MacKenna said we need to report it to them before we'd go down."

"If that implies they'd expect us to go back to the surface to investigate, then it doesn't matter what they want."

"I know," he said, nodding and holding up his hand. "That's a mistake I won't repeat.

"Good," she said.

"Also, in that regard I can safely say Dr. Caldwell did manage to clear us all medically," he said, smiling. "So at least there isn't a problem with exposure."

"Exposure is a legal term too, you know," she said. "There might not be a contagion issue, but there is still a real issue of legal risk."

He nodded. "Though I'd be willing to wager that might not be as bad as you think."

"They cracked the seal on the cargo," she said. "There is no way that is not a big stink."

"Do you know what the cargo is?" he asked.

She shrugged. "I've read the manifest. It's all medical gear and supplies. I don't know what most of it does, but I know med-tech is all valuable, and easily moved on the underground. That means we're in a dangerous area here if anything comes up missing."

"It's research equipment," he said.

"Alright, but that's still not hard to redirect to the dark economy," she said.

"Probably not in this case," he said, fighting not to grin despite the gravity of the situation.

"She raised an eyebrow but waited for him to fill in the missing data.

"Dr. Caldwell is a research associate at the Shan Takhu Institute." He paused to let that sink in. "And we did pick up the cargo modules at Armstrong Station."

"Are you saying that's...?"

He nodded. "Alien hardware."

"Are you sure?" she asked. "I don't know that I've ever heard of alien tech being transported out of Zone One. Especially on a commercial carrier."

"No doubt," he said. "She told me and then Rene confirmed it. All I know is when she tried to explain the scan she did to prove we were clean, I got lost in the first sentence. So did Preston and although he's no doctor, he works hard to keep up on medical science."

"Yah, he's a good kid," she said absently. The realization of what they were actually carrying seemed to be more distressing to her than it was intriguing. She set her fork down and twisted to look at where they were crating another piece of equipment.

"It apparently takes a certain level of highly unique understanding to even hook it up. The way I see it, that means hardware like that is not something that would move well in the underground," he said.

"Maybe," she said. "Or it makes it priceless."

"The other factor here is that although Smythe Biomedical bankrolled her work, the cargo really is hers," he said. "Smythe chose not to list her as steward on the manifest because it would be like painting a target on her. Without her, the hardware is mostly useless junk, and without the junk, she's just another doctor."

"Yah, that's not too uncommon," she said.

"At least the shipper won't be likely to press criminal charges against us for letting her have access," he said.

"Probably not, but it doesn't end the problem." She leaned into her hand and massaged her forehead. "You are right that they likely won't be coming after you for internal piracy charges, although you're looking at a severe violation of company policy, regardless."

"I'm still working on that one."

"Like I said, you're a good captain and I haven't finalized my report yet. When I do file it, I'm going to try to make it as gray as I can, to give you some wiggle room. If you can find a good reason for taking a potential risk, then maybe they will just rub your nose in it and put you in the corner for a while." She shook her head. "Unfortunately, *mitigating circumstances after the fact* is a damned feeble excuse, and a lousy defense."

"One stone at a time," he said.

CHAPTER ELEVEN

THE SHADOW OF SHADETREE crawled across the surface of Starlight as a blanket of darkness, blotting out the blistering heat. The view out the forward view screen should have been fascinating, but instead it seemed like a giant empty hole in reality. The front edge of the eclipse had just reached the colony and Ethan stared at it, hoping to see the lights of the colony coming on in response to the miniature nightfall, but instead there was nothing.

"We're still not getting anything from the surface?" He knew the answer, so the question was pointless.

"No," Marti said.

"We've listened continuously since we got here," Nuko said, shaking her head. "I keep hoping that someone will send up a flare or something. Anything."

He nodded.

"I can't imagine what it's like for Kaycee and Elias," she said. "Not knowing if their families are dead has to be horrible."

He nodded again. Suddenly, the front edge of an idea formed in his mind. "Maybe we're coming at this wrong. We've been looking for signs of life. Maybe we should be looking for signs of death."

"What?"

"We can look for secondary indicators that might imply there was something wrong" he said.

"Our sensors are extremely specialized, Captain," Marti said. "We can scan electromagnetically and gravitationally to a high resolution, but we have limited sensor definition in other areas."

"I know that," he said. "But we do have the capacity to measure chemical composition of the atmosphere, don't we?"

"We have a basic environmental kit," Nuko said.

He nodded. "Bad as it sounds, dead things produce methane."

"The resolution of the scanning technology would be insufficient to detect the methane produced by a decomposing body," Marti said.

"Yah, but a hundred thousand bodies sitting in an oven would produce a lot of it," the captain said. "We know what the atmosphere down there is supposed to be composed of, so if we do the highest accuracy scan we can, shouldn't we be able to pick up elevated levels of things not supposed to be there?"

"Captain, I believe your proposal has scientific merit," it said, almost sounding embarrassed at missing the obvious.

"We're still sitting close to the barycenter between the planets," Nuko said. "It would help to drop into a low orbit and make several sweeps over the colony to increase our scanning accuracy."

"It would increase the resolution exponentially," Marti said.

"Then let's do that and see if we can get some answers," he said.

Nuko pulled her seat up to her console and then paused. "Leigh will know we're moving the ship as soon as I fire up the engines to change orbit," she said. "She's on a thin edge. Do you think this might knock her over again?"

"Probably." Ethan pushed back in his chair and drummed his fingers on the edge of his console. "Do it anyway. I'll explain it to her if she goes sidewise."

"It beats sitting on our thumbs," she said as she punched in the course heading and powered up the engines.

"I don't have thumbs," Marti said.

"Just work with me, you silly girl," Nuko said, shaking her head.

"How many orbits will it take to—?"

"Captain Walker, why are we moving the ship?" the Triple-C said over the open comm. Her voice echoed throughout the ship.

That didn't take long, he thought, shaking his head.

"We're doing a couple recon orbits over the colony to see if we can detect any changes in the environment," he said back over the comm before he sat down in his seat and switched her to a private channel. "I don't want to have this conversation on the shipwide."

"Sorry. I didn't know where you were, and I needed to make sure I got your attention," she said. Her tone shifted from icy to acidic. "By what authority did you order the heading changed?"

"There's no risk to the ship, and I decided that it might be useful to see if there were changes in the atmosphere around the colony," he said. "If there are dead bodies down there, we'll be able to detect methane in the air with our meteorological kit."

"How long will it take to get the results?"

"I don't know, but it's going to take us several low orbits at least," he said.

"Why did you decide to do this now?" she asked.

"Even though we're not doing much, it might be enough to make our passengers feel like we're trying," he explained. It was a lie, because he hadn't thought of it until just then, but it might make her happy. "If we can keep them thinking we're working to get the answers they need, until the *Magellan* gets here, that will make it easier to keep the peace."

She left him hang for several seconds. "I'm not sure I think moving the ship just to mollify the passengers is a good idea, but I won't argue with you. I feel a lot safer with some distance between us and the planet."

"Understood." He didn't, but one good lie deserved another.

"As soon as you've got enough data to work with, get us back to the transfer point." She snapped the comm off from her end and left him chewing on the inside of his lip.

Nuko snorted. "Does she think a virus can leap from the surface and then eat its way through the hull?"

"Viruses are capable of living in a vacuum," Marti said.

"You took a dose of literalicin this morning didn't you?" she said. "It was sarcasm."

"Really? I couldn't tell," the AA said, never missing a beat.

"Children, play nice," the captain said.

"Hey, Boss, Kaycee and Elias are both asking why you're moving the ship," Rene said. "Has something changed down there?" The engineer was still supervising the packing up of the alien tech from the MedBay.

"Nothing that we've picked up, but we're still trying," he said. "We figured if we got closer, then some of the lower resolution systems might give us some clues."

"Understood. You're going to do a gas analysis," he said. "Good thinking. Maybe you can find some more meatloaf while you're at it."

"Exactly," the captain said, wrinkling his nose at the memory. "Leigh gave me a few orbits, but we'll push it as far as we can, so maybe we can get some usable scans."

"I'll pass the word," he said.

"Wait, before you jump, how much longer until they're done?"

"Another couple hours or so," the engineer said. "I can almost see the deck in MedBay now."

"That long?" he asked. "Are they dragging boots down there?"

"They've been busting their spleens, but they had a lot of gear set up," Rene said. "Pruitt told me they also have to let internal power decay before they can safely lock some of it down. I know that with the amount of power they needed to stand this stuff up, they're smart to be cautious when they pack it away."

"Nojo. Just keep me posted," Ethan said, punching the comm off again. He stood back up and stretched, stifling a yawn with the back of his hand. "Before I got interrupted, twice, I was going to ask how many orbits before we will know if something stinks down there?"

"Now look who's being literal," Nuko said, glancing over her shoulder at him and winking.

"If we assume that everyone is dead and in the open air, we will know on the first orbit," Marti said. "However, if the death toll is not 100%, or the bodies are in partly sealed buildings, it may take several overflights."

"And winds might affect how rapidly it dissipates," Nuko pointed out.

"I wasn't too far off then," he said.

"Depending on the situation on the surface, your accuracy was surprising," Marti said.

"Do you need me to watch the deck so you can get some time out of here?" Ethan asked Nuko.

"Oh, hell no," she said, shaking her head. "I like being away from the chaos downstairs."

"Then, if I have time to stand down before we get anything solid, I'll be elsewhere," he said as he turned and headed toward the door.

"You go have fun with that and if anything turns up, I know how to find you," she said.

He needed something to eat, but he was developing an aversion to chaos too, so the mid-deck wasn't where he wanted be. Not that there was a lot of anywhere else he could go.

Ethan ended up wasting time sitting at the desk console in his quarters going over his log files and arguing with himself about how he'd defend his decisions when Leigh's report finally made it back to CSL headquarters. He knew it wasn't helpful to shovel layers of stress over his frustration, but he couldn't imagine what he was going to face when he got home. It was all pointless conjecture.

When he could stand it no more, he logged out of his workstation and made his way down to the mid-deck. It was inviting trouble in the form of unwanted conversation, but he had to eat.

"Everything is crated back up and put away, and we've just retracted the tube," Rene said when he caught him sneaking onto the galley. The engineer followed him in and punched up a cup of pseudojo. "They aren't happy that we're powering it down and locking it down. You can expect to get an earful."

"Thanks for the warning," Walker said, glancing at the chrono on the food printer. "We've only got fifteen hours to go until I can hand them off to Captain MacKenna. From then on she can deal with their garbage."

"Is Leigh drawing up paperwork to transfer them over?"

"I should have her start on it," he said, grabbing his tray and walking over to the one corner of the dining area where he was out of sight from the lift. "The sooner I can get them out of my airspace the better I'll be."

"What about the cargo? I don't think Kaycee will leave it behind and I don't think a multicruiser can carry the modules," Rene said, following him but not taking a seat at the table. "That's a damned lot of stuff to hand-stack over."

"I know," Ethan said. He nodded to the open chair, but Rene shook his head.

"Leigh won't let us leave it parked here either," he said.

The captain tapped his fingers on the edge of the table. "It's twelve days round trip to get a comm back from Smythe, so the good wager says we'll be doing an RTS run to get it back to Armstrong Station at least."

"A Return To Sender means we're eating the cost of both directions," Rene said.

"And it means we're not going to be free of Kaycee for a while," he said.

"Or Elias," the engineer said, tilting his head in the general direction of the lift. "I think I'll leave you two to talk."

When Ethan glanced in the direction Rene had indicated, he knew he should have starved quietly to death in his room.

"Captain, I'd like to make one last appeal to you," the man said as he sat in the chair across the table, uninvited.

Walker shook his head.

"Put yourself in my place," Pruitt said. "I've been away for two years and when I finally make it home, my family and everything I know isn't there."

"I understand your position, but there's nothing I can do," Ethan said. "I'm already facing the real possibility of my career taking an unfortunate turn from just going down there in the first place."

"Nothing personal, but how does that compare?" he said, his voice showing the strain of trying to keep his emotions held inside. It made him very hard to read. "Your career versus my family? As far as we know everyone is dead."

"That's why we moved down to a close orbit," he said, putting the lid back over his meal and sitting back. Glancing across the room to check the time again he shook his head. "Not to be insensitive, but we're looking for methane that would tell us if there are a lot of bodies down there. By this point, we're on our third orbit. The longer it takes us to catch a positive hit, the less likely it is that there's anything dead. We'd know already." He was trying to be reassuring, but it appeared to have the opposite effect.

"If they're not dead, then where are they?" he asked. His tone sounded almost like he was begging for help. It was disturbing to see this mountain of a human on the edge of tears. He stopped himself and looked down.

"I don't know, but I don't think they're dead."

Elias swallowed hard and reset himself emotionally, replacing his despair with a thick veneer of anger. "You're being unreasonable," he said, his voice close to a growl.

"Maybe I am, but this isn't in my control limits anymore," Walker said. He leaned back further in his seat and looked around, spotting Angel and Billy sitting against the far wall. They were watching the exchange intently. "I can't do anything to change the situation. What happens from here on is Captain MacKenna's call. The *Magellan* arrives in the morning and you can take it up with her."

"She'll give me the same runabout you are," he said, balling his fists up and setting them on the edge of the table.

This is about to explode, Ethan thought, wondering how he could get his handlers closer before it did. "The one difference will be that she's got a lot more leeway to interpret things than I do. If I had my way we'd have gone down already, but I can't make that call."

Elias slammed both fists against the table and Ethan jumped back. "Frak! Just give us a shuttle and let us go alone."

"We've been over this. You're not people as far as the company I work for is concerned. You are cargo," he said as his handlers appeared on both sides of Elias and pulled him up out of his seat.

He jerked his arms free. "Sorry," he said, taking a deep breath and struggling to find words. His eyes glassed over and he shook his head. "I have a three-year-old daughter down there. You can't imagine how this feels." He pivoted and walked away.

"Do you want us to lock him down?" Billy asked.

"No," the captain said. "He's right. I can't imagine, so I sure as hell don't want to make it worse."

CHAPTER TWELVE

"Captain, we have a situation developing." Marti's voice sliced through the darkness like a laser.

Ethan snapped up in bed, blinking as his mind struggled to reassemble itself into consciousness. The lights were still off in his room, so it had to be well before his alarm. He'd been dreaming about a small girl. He knew it had to be Elias daughter, or what he imagined her to be, and she was trapped in a cave under an empty dead city. He had been trying to dig his way through rocks and rubble to get to her and every time he pulled one rock away, ten more fell into the opening. The nightmare still held him gripped in its steel claws.

"What?" he croaked. His voice felt like he'd been screaming.

"We have a situation developing," Marti repeated.

He glanced at the illuminated face of his chrono. 0110 hours. "What's the problem?"

"I am detecting that one of our shuttlecraft is missing," it said.

A shuttle is missing? I must still be dreaming. There was no way he'd heard the AA's answer correctly. "Missing? Where is it?"

"Entering the upper atmosphere of Starlight," Marti said.

He groaned, twisting and setting his feet on the floor. Squinting his eyes, he called up the lights and expected to see boulders cascading from the roof of the cave. It had to be part of the dream. *This can't be real.*

"How did that happen?" he asked.

"I do not know," it said, managing to sound embarrassed at not having a good answer.

"How the hell don't you know?" he said. "You don't sleep, and a shuttle can't simply vanish."

"I am uncertain," it said. "I have to assume it is an awareness issue similar to the event that allowed the passengers to access the cargo containers undetected."

Reality snapped into focus around him and he shook his head. *Yes, this has happened before.* "I'm guessing that Elias and Kaycee are in it?" he asked, standing up and grabbing his basic duty coverall out of the dressing cabinet.

"That would be a logical assumption," Marti said. "I cannot locate them anywhere aboard the *Olympus Dawn*."

"Have you tried to hail the shuttle?"

"There was no response," it said.

"Of course not," he said. He could feel his frustration building with each non-answer he got from the AA. "Can you override the controls and bring it back?

"Negative," it said. "The teleoperation link appears to have been taken offline."

Ethan rapped his knuckles on the top of the cabinet for several seconds before he shook his head. *This is going to get twisty fast.*

"Who's awake?" he asked.

"Currently, only you," Marti said.

"Get everyone on deck," he said. "Except Leigh. Tell them all to be quiet. I don't want someone to wake her by accident and having her find out what's going on until I decide what to do."

"I assumed that would be your desire," it said, pausing less than a second before adding, "I have notified all of them."

He only barely got to the ConDeck before Nuko and Rene arrived. Neither of them was completely dressed when they burst through the door.

"What's swinging?" Rene asked as he skidded to a stop on the edge of the riser. "Marti said we've got an emergency situation?"

Nuko crashed into her seat and called up the ship systems screens on her console. "I don't see any problems. The boards all look clear."

"It's not the ship," he said as he punched the situation display up on the main screen. He pointed at the marker icon showing the position of the shuttlecraft as it dropped into the atmosphere. "That's shuttle two."

"Oh frak," Nuko said. "How'd they launch without authorization?"

"I don't see how it would be possible," Rene said. He stepped down behind Ethan and leaned over the back of his chair.

"This is the second time Elias circumvented the surveillance equipment," he said.

"This time he has also overridden several other systems," Marti said.

Rene nodded. "He'd have to at least compromise the launch and approach control system, and the proximity detection grid. Then he'd have to hack a control code to even activate the shuttle's pilot console. That's nearly impossible."

"Obviously not," Walker said, flinging an arm toward the screen. "We need to figure out how he did it."

"Did what?" Angelique Wolfe said as she appeared at the door grinding her fist into an eye and flopping down into one of the observation seats.

"The passengers stole a shuttle," Nuko said.

"That's nogo," she said. "We're frakking in deep now."

The captain nodded, twisting to glance in her direction. "My thought exactly."

"He has to have brought something aboard in his personal stuff that would let him do it," Rene said. "I don't know what it would be, but this isn't a trick you can pull off without high-end tools."

"Angel, go check his gear," Ethan said. "Chances are he took his gear with him, but he might have left other surprises in his stateroom that we need to worry about."

"Yah Boss, cando," she said as she bounced back up and disappeared through the door.

Turning back to Rene, he frowned. "I want you to go over every ship system and figure out what he did. I hate to say it, but I also think it would be a good idea to stick a finger up Marti's ass and see if you can tell if there are other signs of tampering."

"Anatomically that might be problematic," the AA said. The truth was that it took a legal binder to access some parts of Marti's system without its permission. The law considered any AA above level six to be a life form, so without its consent, a human couldn't access any of the primary core systems where its awareness lived.

"Sorry Marti, but we need to be sure you aren't compromised. If you'll give us permission, I think we cannot take the chance," he said.

"I understand. I have done a full diagnostic and although I have discovered no issues, the potential does seem to exist that there have been alterations to my awareness that I cannot detect. Unfortunately, your suggestion has merit," it said. "I will figuratively bend over, so you can accomplish this exam."

"Have you tried to talk them out of this?" Nuko suggested. She was staring at the display like she could turn them around by force of will.

"Marti says they didn't respond to hails before," he said.

"Kaycee likes you," she said. "Maybe you should try it yourself."

At this moment, he wasn't much enamored of the doctor, but Nuko was right. He should give it a shot. He sighed. "Open a channel to the shuttle."

"Signal link established. They are receiving you," Marti said.

"Doctor—"

Nuko shot him an expression that said, '*be friendly.*'

He cleared his throat and started over. "Kaycee. What the hell are you doing?"

She rolled her eyes and shook her head. Obviously, she thought he was hopeless.

Silence answered over the open comm.

"Elias? Either of you? Please answer me," he said, struggling to make his voice sound more worried than pissed. "You've stolen a shuttle and you're about to cross a line we can't walk away from. You need to turn around and we can pretend this never happened."

He glanced at the chrono. "The *Magellan* is just over seven hours from entering the system. You can't be on the surface when they get here. You have to return to the ship, now."

Again, silence filled the ConDeck as they waited.

"I understand you're desperate to find out what's going on, but please don't force me to come get you."

"They've cut the comm from their end," Marti said.

Preston and Billy both stood on the deck having only appeared in the last seconds of the captain trying to talk to the shuttle. That was enough to bring them up to speed.

"Are you up for another excursion to the surface?" Walker asked, looking over his shoulder at the med-tech.

"Excuse me?" Preston asked, his face wrinkling into confusion.

"Yah. Our passengers have escaped, and we need to go get

them," Walker said.

"Right, I figured out that much, but I thought they told us not to go back to the surface," he said.

"Details," the captain said, trying to make light of the idea that he was about to follow them over the line in a huge way.

"I don't think it's a good idea," Nuko said.

"Me either," Ethan said. "I also don't think I've got any choice."

"Boss, you really need to think this through," Rene said. "You've just managed to talk yourself into a survivable position with Leigh. If you go down there again, you're one hundred percent foobed."

"He's right. If you do this, you'll be venting your career," Nuko said, her eyes pleading with him to change his mind. "This time you're not only breaking company policy, you're also disobeying orders from FleetCom. You'll lose the advantage of having the two-ton bear on your side."

"I know that, but what happens to my career if I lose two passengers?" he said. "We don't know what's going on and they could end up dead. I'm stuck between the devil and the deep dark black. I've got to get them back aboard."

"There has to be another way," she said.

"You could let them go and when the *Magellan* shows up, let MacKenna sort out their mess," Rene said.

"And if something happens to them, I'm still liable," he said. "Even if they did steal a shuttle to go kill themselves, I let them get away with it. I don't have time to debate this."

"Boss, I'm in Pruitt's stateroom," Angel interrupted. Even over the comm he could tell she sounded frustrated. "It's empty. He packed out entirely. Looks like he took everything but the bed sheets."

"Copy that," he said. "So, they're not looking to come back."

"I'll check Kaycee's room, but the wager would be she's skipped too," she said.

"Stand by a second."

He turned back to face Billy and Preston. "Do you think you can do another excursion?" he asked.

"Probably," the med-tech said. "I'll go get some gear and meet you in the hangar. I want to make sure we've got the right stuff to deal with the heat."

"Make feet," the captain said. "They've already got a half hour jump on us and I don't want to lose them."

As Preston spun and disappeared, he nodded to Billy. "Are you in?"

The handler nodded. "Far be it from me to let my captain do something questionable without wanting to be part of the fun."

"Angel, are you willing to volunteer for a walkabout in hell?" Walker asked.

"I don't think that's smart, but I'm good for dancing with the devil, as long as he don't start playing fiddle music," she said.

"Good," he said. "You and Billy swing by the hurt locker and tool up for some bondage. We may have to bring them back by force."

"Aye Boss, as you wish." she said.

"I'll meet you on the hangar deck in ten," he said, cutting the comm.

Billy launched himself out the door without waiting for orders and with an almost fiendish gleam in his eye.

He enjoys trouble a bit more than is healthy, Ethan thought. Once the three of them were alone on the ConDeck he shrugged. "Let's hope this all doesn't turn out to be too stupid."

"I think that's unavoidable," Nuko said. She refused to look at him, so she missed the quick glare he shot in her direction.

"You're really going to do this aren't you?" Rene asked.

"If I had any other way to do it—"

"You do," he snapped. "Send Marti down in an automech. At least then you aren't risking your flesh and blood crew. No offense, Marti."

"None taken," it said.

"Marti, could you guarantee that whatever magic voodoo Elias has going on, wouldn't override control of your skinsuit?" Ethan asked.

"Unfortunately, because I do not understand what he has done so far, I cannot," the AA said.

"That settles it," he said, pushing back from his console and standing up.

"Then let me lead the excursion," Rene said. "If you stay up here, you can at least say I did it without permission."

He shook his head. "You need you to figure out what he did, so that when I get his ass back here, he can't do it again."

"We can just keep him locked up and away from whatever tools he used to make it happen," the engineer said. "Please. Let me do this."

"No," Ethan said. "If nothing else I need you up here because you're the only one still on speaking terms with Leigh. She'll go shitblind pissed when she finds out I've gone to the surface. I don't care how you do it, but you've got to buy me as much time as you can. Take the deep-comm offline if you need to."

"Taking the transmitter offline is a violation of safety protocol," Marti said.

"I know," he said. "Just do what you can to get me the chance to bring them back. Who knows, if I get lucky, maybe I'll make it back before she wakes up and calls in my firing squad."

CHAPTER THIRTEEN

THE APPROACH WAS ROUGH, but Ethan was trying to make up for lost time and came in as hot as the shuttle would handle. As it was, they were a full hour behind Kaycee and Pruitt when they screamed low over the outer buildings of the colony. It was almost sunset local time, even though it was still well before firstshift on the *Olympus Dawn*, so although it meant they didn't have long to wait until it cooled down, they were coming in at the absolute worst part of the afternoon.

Before they made their final approach, Marti had updated their destination. "They've landed outside what looks to be a large administrative building. There are markings that appear to indicate it is a hospital complex."

"That figures. She'd want to go to ground in a place she knows well. That'll give her the home field advantage," Angel said. She sat in the rear seat adjusting the sling on a laser rifle. He'd ordered them to leave the lethal force armament in the shuttle once they got to ground, but neither of his handlers liked that idea. They'd packed enough firepower to invade the planet, but when he reminded them that killing their cargo was a bad idea, they both agreed to carry stun-pellet pistols.

"The hospital is also the place with the highest risk if it is a contagion," Preston said, glancing back and nodding. "If it turns out to be a disease."

"Shuttle Two is approximately 150 meters outside the main entrance to the facility in a cleared area that may be a medical transport pad," Marti said.

"Is there room for us to put down there?" the captain asked.

"Affirmative," it said, superimposing a visual feed from orbit onto the corner of their main screen. The clearing was large enough to land a dozen small ships.

"Are they still inside the shuttle?" he asked.

"As far as I can tell from the lack of EM signal, it is powered down," the AA said. "I doubt they would remain long in the ship without life support systems to keep it cool."

"Agreed, but I want to come in fast and low anyway, just to make sure they don't see us coming." He glanced out the window and nodded. "Cinch up the belts. Here we go."

Flipping their shuttle belly-over, he used the undercarriage to add aerodynamic drag to their forward motion and bring their speed down without the engines. The ship groaned under the stress, but they screamed to a stop almost directly above the other ship. As he dropped the twenty meters to the ground, he could see the hatch open on the smaller shuttle. It was clear there was no one inside.

The landing gear extended, and they hit the ground with a bouncing hop. "Sorry that was choppy," Walker said.

"As long as she'll get us home." Billy unsnapped his belt, twisted around to grab his pistol out of the locker behind him. He also pulled out a laser rifle, and the captain shook his head.

"We've already covered this. Leave the big guns here."

"But—"

"Technically they are still our passengers," he said. "Stun pellets will do the job and leave me with a much smaller mess to clean up."

"Lasers are clean. Do you seriously want to chance letting Pruitt go hands on?" Billy asked, looking skeptical at the captain's decision.

"You don't think seventy-five thousand volts will drop him?" he asked.

"Billy's just a big coward," Angel teased.

He gave her an old-fashioned gesture about her sexual proclivities and then bounced for the airlock door. The gravity was about eighty percent standard and between that and his apparent adrenaline, he almost overshot and narrowly missed smashing into the ceiling.

"You might want to wait a second," Preston said, tossing him a bag of water. "Wet your clothes down. It will help." He pitched a second one at Angel.

"Is it that bad out there?" she asked.

"Worse," Ethan said, nodding and taking a bag from the med-tech. He tore the end off and poured it over his head and down the front and back of his coveralls.

"Current outside temperature is sixty-six degrees," Marti said.

"Holy frak! Seriously?" Billy stopped and stepped back from the door like he expected to find demons waiting on the other side.

"I don't drink my pseudojo that hot," Angel said as she also ripped her water open and poured it over her head.

"At this level, the heat will be close to deadly in short order," Preston said. "We need to not waste any time outside. Especially not in the direct sunlight."

"Problem is it might be almost as bad inside the buildings," the captain said. "When we swing the hatch, you'll need to be looking for shade as quick as you can." He pointed out the front window toward a wide veranda that ran the length of the building and concealed the main entrance.

"Is that where they went in?" she asked, leaning forward and dripping water from her hair onto the back of the pilot seat.

"I am unable to tell, but I am uncrating my automech and will proceed there first before stopping to scan," Marti said. The sound of hardware shuffling in the lock came through the closed hatch.

"I want to see if I can recover their shuttle," the captain said. "I'll duck in there and check if I can do anything, so I'll be a minute or so behind you all."

"I'll stay with you," Billy said.

"No. I'll do this on my own. I know they aren't in the shuttle," he said. "They'll be inside the building somewhere. I want you two to be ready to snag them if they saw us come in and stick their heads back out to see what we're doing."

"Cando," Angel said. The sounds of the automech squeezing through the door diminished and its shadow passed over one of the side ports.

"Let's move," the captain said as he pulled the inner door open and gasped. The residual heat from when the AA had moved its skinsuit out, lingered like an oven in the airlock. "Grab a visor and go. Don't bother closing the inner door. Leave it open and clear out."

"I will close it behind you," Marti said, reminding him that it still had teleoperation control of their shuttle if needed. Or convenient.

Preston took a deep breath and nodded as he leaped up and pushed out on the heels of the handlers.

Grabbing an emergency tool kit from the small locker under the pilot's seat Walker jumped through the lock and out onto the dry ground. The moss like grass covering crackled under his boots and he looked down at it as he reached back in and grabbed his visor. It was the same grassy plant life that had been in the backyard of the House of Terrifying Meatloaf, but instead of being living and pliable, this was dead and decomposing to dust.

"Captain, do not waste time," the AA said over the commlink in his visor.

"Roger that," he said, darting into the shade of the other shuttle's open hatch. He stopped his forward velocity with an outstretched hand and immediately regretted it as the metal edge of the doorway seared his exposed skin.

"Shit!" he roared, looking at the red scalded skin on his palm. "Don't touch anything with a bare hand."

"Boss, do you need help?" Preston asked. "I can come back out there—"

"Negative, stay in the shade and let me get this done," he said. He flipped open the tool kit and grabbed a glove for his good hand. He didn't want to put anything on the burned one, so he fumbled trying to get the good one protected as he looked around. The air inside the shuttle almost vibrated with heat.

Stepping up to the pilot console, he took a gloved finger and tapped the activation icon. Miraculously the system lit up. He glanced over at the communications panel and tapped it. It also came on. "Marti, it looks like it's powering up," he said as he fired up the life support controls. Cool air blasted out of the overhead recycler duct.

"I have a telemetry uplink," the AA said. "I am testing the teleoperation system now."

The floor plates vibrated and the artificial gravity shuddered several times as standard grav and the local gravity flickered on and off. "That doesn't feel right," Walker said. He held his blistered hand up in front of the cold air coming out of the vent while he waited for the ship to power up the rest of the way.

"The artificial gravity system is above safe thermal limit and will not establish," Marti said through the shuttle's comm system. "Otherwise I have full control of all systems."

"So, you can fly this one home?"

"If you wish me to," it said.

"Yah," he said, glancing out the side window at their other shuttle. "No wait. I want you to take both shuttles up to 300 meters and keep them there. Hopefully, that will put them both out of reach of Pruitt's whatever-it-is. Then if we need them, you've got them preflight ready and on standby to get us out of here."

"Understood, Captain. As soon as you are clear, I will remove both shuttles from the landing zone."

"If there's any question whether you can maintain control of either shuttle, move them as far away as necessary to protect them." Looking around, he nodded. Taking a last deep breath of the already cooler air, he threw himself back out the door and trotted toward the hospital. He was about halfway across the distance when he heard the nearly subsonic thrum of the shuttles launching into the air.

Preston had his medkit open and was holding a tube of skinseal and a wet cloth in his hands when the captain skidded to a stop on the veranda. Grabbing Ethan's hand and twisting it so he could look at the burn, the med-tech flipped his exam visor over his eyes with a toss of his head.

"It's a mild second-stage burn," he said, after several seconds. "You've got minor cellular damage to the skin. It's not too serious, but it'll hurt for a while."

He put the damp biogauze over the red area and reached down into his kit for a sprayer. "This will numb it until we can get up to the ship and do a regen on it."

"It's not that bad," the captain said, frowning as he pulled his hand away and lifted the gauze.

The med-tech snagged it back and gave him a surprisingly firm glare. "If you want to put a glove on this hand so you don't burn it again, you have to let me treat it," he said.

"Yes sir," the captain said, grinning and winking at Angel who was snickering. Preston was young, and although none of them admitted it to his face, they all respected his medical skill.

"What do we know?" the captain asked as he waited for the med-tech to finish doctoring his hand.

"Inside temperature is nine degrees lower than ambient outside," Marti said, using its local audio channel on the automech. "Once your repairs are complete, I recommend we proceed inside."

"That's still damned hot but is there power on inside?" he glanced toward the horizon where the red disk of Kepler-186 was just edging toward the top of the tallest buildings in the distance.

"I do not detect electromagnetic fields, so I doubt that is the case," it said. "The building appears to have several sub floors and convection is pulling cooler air from underground, up through the central core of the building. It appears this was an element of the structure's design."

"Do you detect any life signs?"

"Negative," it said. "The building itself has major metallic components in the sub floors that limit my effective scanning range."

"Boss, they got inside through here," Billy hollered from where he stood in front of a different section of the hospital face. Signs in the overhead said it was the triage department. "It looks like someone pried a service door off the tracks."

"You think it was them?"

"It's hard to tell. It's a huge door, but there are boot prints in the dust," he said. "Fresh ones."

"You're good to go as soon as the skinseal cures," Preston said, snapping his kit closed and smiling. His coating of water had already dried and sweat was turning his jumpsuit dark around his collar and across his chest.

At least he's sweating this time.

"Let's get inside and out of the heat," Walker said, jerking his head in Billy's direction.

"Like fifty-seven is cool," Preston said.

"It's all relative," Angel said.

CHAPTER FOURTEEN

INSIDE THE DOORWAY, a large space opened onto a reception area. Several desk consoles, each with an attached diagnostic archway, lined an entire wall of the room. It was dark and lifeless with only a sliver of orange light slicing across the floor from the broken door to provide illumination.

"This was obviously a medevac receiving area," Preston said as he walked toward one of the desks. He clicked on a handbeam and scanned the area behind and under the workstation.

"Why do you say that?" Billy asked.

"No signs," he said, flashing his light around the room. "That tells me that anyone coming through the door here would know where they're headed, and what they're looking at. Public areas always have signs directing traffic to the reception desk and waiting areas."

"Good catch," Ethan said. "This would be familiar territory for Kaycee?"

"Not necessarily," Marti said as it turned on a set of high-power lights that illuminated the entire room. "Dr. Caldwell is a Medical Research Doctor and may have no triage specialty background."

"While she was treating me for my sunstroke, she told me

she'd done time as an intern in an emergent care hospital," Preston said. "But she also said there were three hospital facilities in Starlight."

"Would they all have the same floor plan?"

"Who knows," he said.

"Standardized design modules would mean similar functional elements, but there could be substantial variation to address specialized services," Marti said.

"So, we know that gives them an edge, but we don't know how big an edge it is," Billy said.

"Now that we're inside, can you scan anything else?" the captain asked, walking over to the automech and grabbing bags of water from its carrying rack. He tossed each of them one and they all hosed themselves down again. It didn't help as much this time since the water was warmer than fresh urine, but evaporation would eventually kick in and cool them off a little. Hopefully.

"At this point I can tell that there are at least four sub-floors beneath us," it said, shining a beam toward an open doorway.

Kaycee said there were emergency shelters under the hospitals and municipal buildings," he said. "Is that what you're seeing?"

"The air appears to be several degrees cooler deeper inside the building," it said. "It would be logical to assume that the shelters would be built far enough underground to maintain temperature. If they are seeking survivors, this would be where they would look. The environment is certainly more conducive to this possibility."

"The tracks head in this direction," Angel said. "But the dust gets thinner further from the door. If they don't step in something to make a mess, it's going to get harder to track them from footprints."

"Are you picking up any carrier signals from commlinks?" Ethan said.

"Negative," Marti said.

"Chances are they went this way. Since we don't know what they're looking for, other than cool air and survivors, this seems like the only path that makes sense," Angel said.

"I believe proceeding deeper into the building is a sound decision," the AA said.

"Agreed," Walker said.

"I will take point," Marti said, retracting its legs and arms to squeeze through the door as it crabbed forward into the narrow hallway.

"Are you sure you'll fit?" Billy asked as he watched it duck down and push the door open wider with one of its heavy arms.

"I am designed to fit through any standard human egress," the AA said.

"This looks like an administrative section," the captain said as he followed the automech into the hallway. "It's all offices and conference rooms."

Marti marched toward the opposite end of the corridor with its legs partially retracted, bouncing forward like a tap dancing spider on stims. It was effective, but strange and amusing to watch.

"Shouldn't we check the rooms as we go by?" Billy suggested as he and Angel both paused to open the first doors they passed.

"You may do so if you wish, but I am scanning them," it said, stopping and turning its head to focus one of its eyes back at the handler. "Unless I encounter a shielded area or other obstruction to my sensors, it will not be necessary to investigate those locations manually."

"I just don't think it would be good to let them get behind us," he said.

"I think we'd be better off pushing forward as fast as possible," Ethan said. "If they're checking rooms as they go, our advantage is Marti's scanners. Let's not waste that." He didn't want to take any longer than necessary to catch Kaycee and Pruitt. He was painfully aware that the longer it took, the less likely he was to keep things with his Triple-C from blowing up. Every minute wasted down here, was one more that could send his career permanently into the pit.

Angel had walked ahead and was rounding a corner at the end of the hall. "There appears to be a lift shaft here," she hollered back. "The door is closed but there are scuff marks on it."

"Like it's been pried open?" the captain asked as the rest of them joined her on the lift landing.

"Yah," she said as she set her hands against it and pushed it sidewise. It moved, and a blast of cooler air washed out of the empty space beyond the open door.

"That's amazing," Preston said, sighing and stepping forward to enjoy the sensation.

She let the door go and it slammed shut with a thump, leaving the med-tech with a soul shattering look of disappointment on his face. "It's spring loaded," she said. "That's why it closed behind them. There's probably a safety lock they had to break to get it open the first time."

"Can you force it to stay open? I don't want to risk getting trapped on the other side," Walker said.

Marti reached out and drove the manipulator end of one of its heavy arms through the wall, sending them all jumping away in surprise. Tearing out a steel framing member, it handed it to Angel. "This will work," it said.

Shaking her head and laughing, she wedged the beam into the open door and stomped it down against the door sill to drive it into place. Flipping on her handbeam, she leaned into the opening and pointed the light down the shaft. "I don't see the platform, but it only looks to go down a few floors. Maybe twenty meters tops."

"Too far to jump," Billy said. He stood behind the automech, still looking back like he expected someone to come out of one of the doors they'd passed.

"If we've got a tether, we could tie off there," she said. She was shining her light up at the bottom of the lift deck one floor above them.

"We're sure they went this way?" Preston asked, walking around to the small storage box built into the back of Marti's body to look for a rope.

"There is no cable in my kit," it said before he managed to look.

"I don't think we were expecting to be rappelling when we tooled up for this mission," the captain said. "Unless they had a better plan than we do, I don't think they were carrying that kind of gear either."

"Maybe there are handholds," Angel said, grabbing Marti's arm and swinging into the shaft with her upper body to look back at the wall inside the door. "Yah, there's a ladder, and it's got footprints on it."

"I may not be able to traverse a ladder," Marti said, almost sounding disappointed.

Ethan nodded. "Maybe there's another way down—"

"Ethan Walker, are you down on the surface?" Leigh barked over his private command-comm channel. He flinched in surprise.

Frak! "No. You are having a bad dream," he said. "Go back to bed. It will all be better when you wake up."

Muting his mic, he growled and thumped a knuckle against Marti's automech. "Why didn't you tell me she was on to me?"

"I didn't think you needed the distraction at this moment," it said. "In typical unpredictable human fashion, she accessed the commlink without warning."

"Fine. Just figure out how to get us down there," he said, pointing down the shaft and cutting himself back into the comm.

"Are you ignoring me?" she said, her voice sounding like she was fast approaching hysterical. "I can't believe you'd actually be insane enough to do this."

"Leigh, calm down. I had no choice," he said.

"You had no reason. None," she screeched. "It doesn't matter how you try to justify this, there's no way this isn't going to end your career."

"I know you're probably right," he said, stepping back as Marti scuttled forward and tilted its sensor head toward the shaft. "When I get back up there, I'll explain."

"You will explain it to me now," she ordered. "While you are getting back to the shuttle and back to the ship."

"I'm sure Nuko or Rene has told you what happened. I'm down here trying to find our passengers and bring them—"

A bright arcing flash lit the walls with twisted shadows, and then everything plunged into sudden darkness as a thundering crash cut her off in mid sentence.

"Holy frakking hell!" Angel roared.

Blinking several times to clear the spots from his vision, he could see a glow where the body of the automech had flown back and crashed into the wall beside him. The top of its neck was glowing molten red with rivulets of metal slag running down across the floor in hissing rivers of flame. The entire sensor head was gone, like it had been vaporized.

"Everybody report," Walker ordered, ignoring the voice of Leigh screaming in his ear for the moment. He stomped on the flaming carpet trying to put out the tiny fires before they spread.

"We're good," Billy said. A beam of light snapped on behind Marti's body and a second later, another one appeared.

"Speak for yourself," Preston groaned. "You damn near … oh. Never mind." Until he turned around, he'd apparently not seen the dead automech lying in a crumpled heap where he'd just been standing.

"Angel, you still with us?"

"Yah, I'm fine. I'm seeing spots and hanging by my fingers, but unhurt," she said. "I lost my light down the shaft somewhere."

"What the hell happened?" Nuko cut in on the comm overriding the link from Salazar. "Marti says its teleop link has blown out and it can't reestablish a connection to the automech."

"Affirm," Walker said. "Let me get everybody back on their feet and we'll figure that out. Stand by."

Flipping his own handbeam on, he edged toward the open doorway. The air hung heavy with the smell of burned metal and ozone. Leaning into the shaft he spotted Angel dangling from a cable a meter past the doorway. She could have swung over on her own, but with Marti's head exploding in her face, she probably couldn't see it. Reaching in, he grabbed Angel by the front of her jumpsuit and pulled her back into the corridor. She leaned against the wall and slid down to the floor.

Squatting down in front of her he studied her face as he tried not to shine his light directly into her eyes. She had what looked like moderate flash burns and her eyes were pouring water. "Can you see?"

"For the most part," she said. "Fortunately, I wasn't looking right at Marti when it happened."

"Was it a weapon of some kind?" Billy asked as he and Preston climbed over the back of the automech and joined them.

"I don't know," she said, wiping away the tears with the back of her hand. "I was getting ready to swing around and head down the ladder when Marti leaned into the shaft. All I know is it went spastic and then disappeared. After that I was dangling in space and seeing spots."

"Looks like whatever it was, flatlined Marti's body," Billy said, shining his light at the metal carcass.

"Maybe not," the AA said over the commlink from the ship. "If one of you can reset the unit, I might be able to assess the damage and restore some control function."

A diagram of the automech body appeared on his visor screen and Ethan pulled it back over his eyes to study it. The same display must have appeared on Billy's visor, because he flipped it down and climbed up on the carcass to feel around between its legs for the reset switch. "Got it," he said, after several seconds. "They couldn't have put that in a less embarrassing place to get to, could they?"

The automech shuddered violently, and the handler jumped back as it fumbled around trying to find itself. "It appears that all fine-level motor controls are down, however gross system function appears to be restoring. Ambulation should be possible."

"Can you tell what happened?" the captain asked. Preston tapped him on the shoulder, and he stood back up to give him the space in front of Angel.

"Primary power is down to three percent," Marti reported. "I would surmise that I got my head caught in another one of those power-drain fields. Internal diagnostics are telling me that the entire sensor array is offline."

"It slagged your face right the hell off, is more like it," Billy said. "The entire upper surface of your body is covered in molten burn spots and the top half meter of your neck assembly might have vaporized."

"Understood," it said. "At this point I am effectively blind and deaf. I am also critically low on power and will need to return to a shuttle to recharge."

"You can still walk?"

One leg twitched in response. "I have accurate positional awareness and can retrace my course to our landing site. It will take me several hours to recharge fully, but once I have done that, we can resume our mission."

"We can't afford to wait for you to recharge, and even if we did, you'd still be blind without major repairs."

"This is valid," it said. "Without seeing the extent of the damage I do not know if repairs can be made on location."

"I'd say it's a safe wager the answer is no," Walker said. "Do you have enough power to make it back to the shuttle?"

"Yeeezzz," it said, using the local audio. Its voice sounded like it was coming through the blades of a ventilator turbine. With a groan like twisting metal, it pushed itself up off the floor. One leg hung lifeless and drug with a scraping noise as it moved.

"Marti, you're foobed hard," Billy said. "You need to sit this one out. We can go it alone from here."

"Agreed," the captain said, looking down at Angel. "Should she go back too?"

Preston nodded, but Angel glared at him. "I'm good to go," she said. I've got to go get my flashlight.

"Is it safe to go back into the shaft?" Ethan asked.

"It didn't affect me," Angel said.

"Or her handbeam," Billy pointed out. He was looking down the shaft. "It's still working down there. And our passengers apparently went down the ladder with no ill effects either."

"It is possible that the drain only affects high power level systems," Marti said. "In both cases when I was affected, it only activated when one of my core power lines broke a known physical boundary."

"Then you go back and recharge, and we'll press on," the captain said.

"You will not," Leigh said. "You need to get your ass back to

119

the ship now."

He shook his head. "Nuko, lock her in her quarters until I get back to the ship."

"Ethan Walker you wouldn't dare," Salazar snarled.

After several seconds Rene came on the comm. "At this point it probably doesn't matter, but I didn't know Nuko could move like that. I think Leigh's arm will grow back. Eventually."

"Nojo?" the captain asked.

"Mostly nojo. Do what you need to do. The *Magellan* will be dropping out of cruise in about two-and-a-half hours. It would be good for you to be back before I have to make excuses to Captain MacKenna."

"Working on it."

CHAPTER FIFTEEN

THEY WERE FOLLOWING FOOTPRINTS in the dust on the rungs of the ladder. It looked like they'd gone all the way down to the bottom. They didn't want to assume that to be a fact, so the four of them moved slowly in the near total darkness. Every three or four rungs they stopped to make sure they could see evidence that Kaycee and Pruitt had continued.

Relatively speaking it was cooler the further underground they went. And ventilation shafts pulled the air from the lift-shaft outward in directed rivers of almost tolerable cool.

"Wait, I hear something," Preston whispered, as he lingered by one of the vent entrances sucking up the breeze. He cocked his head to the side and held it close to the grating.

"Is it them?" Walker asked from above him on the ladder. He leaned back and looked down between his feet at the med-tech.

"I don't know. It didn't sound like either of them," he said. "But it was definitely a voice." He shook his head.

Angel pointed the light that Billy had loaned her down the ladder. "They went past this level," she said. "At least another floor below me."

Preston's head was just below floor level between sub-level three and four, almost three meters above where she hung. He pointed at the vent with his free hand. "There's someone on this level."

The captain squeezed down beside him. Wrapping an arm around the vertical bar to stabilize, he leaned out and pointed his light down the duct. Side vents broke off every dozen meters or so and slanted up toward the deck above them.

Then he heard it. "That sounds like a kid's voice," he whispered.

The med-tech nodded.

"Billy, see if you can pry the doors on that landing open," Walker said, hitting the inner latch mechanism with the light from his handbeam.

"Boss we're here to find the passengers, not mount a rescue mission," Angel said. "The *Magellan* is coming to deal with that kind of operation."

"She's right," Rene said. "You haven't got time to be a hero."

They were right, but it wasn't in him to leave children behind. He looked down the shaft and then back at the door above, torn between what he should do and what he had to do. Billy hung beside the door waiting for a decision.

"Do it," the captain said. He glanced down at Angel. "We'll take five minutes and if we don't find them, we'll get back after Kaycee and Pruitt."

"It's your career," she said, starting back up as Billy shoved the door open and jumped into the dark opening.

"Yah. It's already over anyway, but at least ending on an up-note is better than whimpering out at the end," he said as he pulled himself up onto the deck.

"What kind of place is this?" Angel said as she stepped out of the shaft behind them.

Preston had walked forward and was looking at the dark control panels along the wall. Several heavy looking metal doors stood closed along the opposite wall. "It looks like a high energy diagnostic facility maybe," the med-tech said. "There are fields of medicine that still use radiologic materials to diagnose and treat diseases."

"Like uranium?" Billy asked as he stepped back from a door he was about to try prying open.

"No, usually things a lot safer than that, but they still require special handling and storage," he explained. "They build shielded rooms to protect the technicians that are exposed all the time from building up a cumulative dose level."

"So, it's safe?" Billy asked his skepticism evident in his tone.

"For the most part," Preston said. "Anything you shouldn't mess with should have clear labels."

"Where are your voices?" Angel said, shining her handbeam down the long room. Other than a couple chairs along the wall, and a wide alcove about halfway to the far end, it was just a wide corridor like most any other in a hospital. We're on a timeline here."

"Spread out and let's see if we can hear them again," the captain said.

"We don't want to pry every door open if we don't have to," Preston said. "The walls will be thick so listen close."

They started down the hall, rapping on doors and listening for a response. Angel made it first to the alcove at the mid-point in the corridor and stopped, shining her light on the wall. "This is odd," she said.

"Whatcha got?" Billy asked. He was almost to the opposite end of the room but had been walking along the wall on the left where most of the doors were. They appeared to be the actual diagnostic and treatment chambers.

"It looks like somebody tried to seal up a door here. It's been plastered over with something," she said.

Walker was staring at a heavy steel door on the opposite wall. Wiping sweat out of his eyes, he was thinking about giving up the search, and going back to chasing his passengers down. He bounced across the hallway and stopped as Angel stepped back abruptly after shining her light around a small workstation in the center of an alcove. A pile of canisters sat in a corner. All of them marked with radioactive materials warning labels.

"That looks like it was the secure supply locker," Preston said as he joined them.

She spun the light back to the plastered over door.

"And that would be thermoplast," the med-tech said, identifying the material plastered over the door.

"Why would they empty the storage room and then seal it up?" she asked. "Unless they were trying to protect something more important than that shit is dangerous." She leaned forward and pressed her ear against the door. After several seconds, she shook her head, pulled out her sidearm, and rapped hard against the center of the door with its handgrip.

This time when she pushed her head against the door she nodded and smiled. "Oh yeah, they're in there. Sounds like a bunch of them."

"How do we get them out? We didn't bring construction tools,"

"I have just begun to recharge my body, but I can attempt to return to your location," Marti said.

"You're blind," the captain said.

"I can mount a body optic from one of the EVA suits to my frame and use that to provide rudimentary vision," it said.

"How much power do you have?" he asked.

"I am back to seven percent," Marti said. "I have one leg actuator that is damaged so mobility is limited, but I can do this."

"How long will it take to bolt on an eyeball?" Ethan asked.

"It will depend on my ability to make the necessary modifications with only one fine-motor arm operating," it said. "I would estimate it may take as much as an hour."

"Get started and we'll look for something to use down here," he said.

Billy had dumped the contents off of a small utility cart and was ripping the handle off by brute force.

"The door is steel, and the wall looks to be polycon," Angel said. "This will take some time."

"And in this heat, it will be even worse," Walker nodded.

"Maybe we can just crack the plaster-stuff off and then force the door," she said.

"It's carbon fiber reinforced polymer," Preston said. "The only way I know of to remove it is to get it to unlink molecularly. It's not supposed to be breakable."

"How do you do that?" Angel asked.

"Normally you use a photo-reactive chemical," he said. "It's specially designed so that when you bombard it with UV light it dissolves the thermoplast."

"Unless you're carrying one of those in your medkit, I don't think that's a possibility," Walker said.

He shook his head.

"How thick do you think the wall is?" he asked as Billy returned with the metal bar and started at the door with the fury of a jackhammer.

"Ten to twenty centimeters minimum," the med-tech said. "But polycon is softer than thermoplast."

"It sure would have been nice to have a laser about now," Billy said as he stopped to adjust his target to the wall surface. "Might be faster to go get it and come back."

"Especially since there's likely to be a metal inner surface once we get through the softer stuff of the wall," Preston said. "They tend to overbuild radiologic lockers."

The handler turned to look at Walker. "I can be back in five minutes," he said.

"Do it," he said, nodding.

Billy took off for the lift shaft at a dead run.

"While he's doing that, I can try to get in through the air vent," Preston suggested. "Once he gets back, it will take a while to burn through the door. I should make sure they're all safe behind stuff before he starts cutting."

"I should do it," Angel said.

"I'm smaller than you," the med-tech said, pointing out the obvious.

"Yah, and if the locker's secure, it'll have reinforced vents inside," she said. "If it's going to take brute meso, I'm your man ... sort of."

Walker thought about it for several seconds before he sighed. "Just be careful."

"Always am," she said as she turned and trotted off. "I'll comm when I'm inside and get the lay of the deck."

"Go with her and see if she needs any help getting into the duct from the shaft," he said, flashing the light down the hall behind her.

The truth was, he just wanted a minute to deal with his thoughts. It didn't matter what was in there, whether it was kids or whatever, he'd flushed everything into the recycler. "Damn it, I know I'm doing the right thing here, but it's foobed no matter how it plays out," he whispered.

"We all know that Ethan," Rene said over the command channel. "Maybe you'll get lucky and this will outweigh the frakking downside."

"That's not why I'm doing it," he said. It surprised him to realize that it wasn't why he was doing it. Although he didn't know exactly why he'd gotten himself in this deep.

"Real heroes never do it to be heroic," Nuko said, joining in.

"She's in the vent," Preston hollered from the far end of the hall. "It's going to be tight, but she should be able to reach them."

"Keep an eye on her in case she runs into trouble," he yelled back, leaning his forehead against the door.

"Boss, I'm outside, the sun's gone down," Billy said. "Where the hell are the shuttles?"

"You weren't paying attention before we got inside were you?" he said. "Look up."

"Got it," he said. "Marti bring our shuttle down please."

"I'm almost there," Angel said. She was grunting as she crawled along the duct. "Oh shit, it stinks in here. In a bad way."

"When you're inside, link in your optic to the comm. I want to see what we're looking at."

He looked down at his belt and realized his visor was missing. He must have taken it off after the energy drain lobotomized Marti and Billy had done the hard reset to get it operating again. "Frak. Preston do you still have your visor with you? I think I left mine upstairs."

"Yah, Boss I'm on my way," the med-tech said.

"This is bad," Angel said, her voice sounding like she'd just swallowed a shot of radiator varnish. "There are a crap ton of kids in here. It looks like more than a few of them didn't make it, but there are at least ten that are still alive. They're all in bad shape."

"Oh, holy frak," Preston whispered as he collapsed against the edge of the counter in front of the door. He had his visor on and was looking at the heads-up display. He peeled it off. His hand shook as he handed it to the captain.

"I think there's at least a dozen dead," she said. He could hear her swallowing hard as she tried to keep her voice steady. "Some of them have been gone a long while."

"You really don't want to do that," the med-tech said, shaking his head and whipping sweat from his pale forehead as Ethan pulled the visor's headband into place.

"It looks like they had a few days' supplies when they were locked in," she said. "But from what I can tell they haven't had any in a while. It's bad. Stand by."

The captain lowered the visor over his eyes and blinked as he focused on the image coming in from her optic. She seemed to be kneeling in front of a young boy. He was at most seven standard years old, but he had eyes that looked a hundred. They were dry and caked with grime. He blinked slowly as she shined her light at him.

"He looks to be the oldest one still alive," she said.

"Can you tell me your name?" she asked, reaching up and brushing the hair out of his face with a gentle hand. He licked his lips and his tongue stuck to the dry and cracked edge of his mouth.

"Miguel," he whispered. "You aren't my mommy. Is she outside?"

"I don't know, Miguel," she said softly. "My name is Angel."

"Are you here to take me away, too?" he asked, nodding. "Momma told me that if she couldn't come back, the angels would come."

CHAPTER SIXTEEN

"Billy if you're still at the shuttle, bring all the water you can carry," Captain Walker said. "And hurry."

"Cando," he said. "Will slow me down a bit, but it looks like there's a front entrance for the radiological medicine department. It might be shorter to come in that way."

"Yah we can check that out once we get them out of the room. I don't want you to waste time fighting your way through locked doors or on potential dead ends," he said. "Just make feet."

"On my way," he said.

"Marti, once he gets clear, get both shuttles as close to that front door as possible," Ethan said. "We're going to be evacuating the survivors and we'll come out that way if it's shorter."

"Yes, Captain," it said. "I will also discontinue repairs to my automech and focus on recharging as quickly as possible so I can provide transportation assistance."

"Nuko, you and Rene get the MedBay ready," he said. "And we'll need mattresses brought up to the mid-deck from the staterooms. Do what you can to get it set up as emergency facilities."

"The *Magellan* will be better equipped," the engineer said.

"They won't be in system for a couple hours yet," he said.

"Once they drop out of cruise, they can't do better than local safe speed. A multicruiser is big and can't risk bending that limit, so they're looking at twelve hours from when they get over the threshold before they can make planetfall."

"That's best case, if we tell them the situation is critical," Nuko added. "If they come in at standard speed, they're almost another day from the drop-in point."

"Yah," Ethan said, realizing the situation wouldn't get any better for him from here on. "We'll have to let them know what we've found. I'm thinking from what we're seeing down here, every second might be critical. We need to get these kids helped before then. Once MacKenna drops into K-186, send her the update. When she rendezvous with us, we can hand them over, but for now it's all our mess."

"Copy that, Boss," Nuko said. Her voice told him that she knew what he'd just ordered her to do would be the last knot in his noose. "We'll be as ready as we can."

"Angel, I need you to do a basic triage in there, so we know who is most critical first. Cando?"

"Yah, Boss. Right now, it looks like we've got four breathing, but unresponsive. I'd bet they're the most critical. One of them looks to be less than two standard years old."

"There's no adult in there at all?"

"There was. I didn't find her body when I first came in. It looks like the children tried to cover her with stuff when she died. It's not …" her voice trailed off. And he could hear her breathing hard. "I don't think it's something I want to keep poking into."

"Understood," he said. "We'll get you all out of there as quick as we can."

"I don't think any of them are strong enough to walk. We will have to carry them all."

"How many are there?"

"I've got four of them alert enough to be talking and asking questions," she said. "Five more of them are too weak to move, but able to respond when I talk to them. Then there are the four that are breathing but not reacting to anything."

"How many didn't make it?"

"Fourteen kids and the adult, I think" she said. "There are stacks of things in here and I don't know what else might be buried."

"We'll need to bring them out too," Walker said.

"I think we should leave that to the *Magellan*," Angel said. "Seriously you don't want to do that."

"She's right," Preston said. "Until they can figure out what happened it's probably best to rescue the survivors and then let someone further up the food chain deal with that."

Billy skidded to a stop at the desk. He'd come up at a dead run and had the bottom half of an EVA suit tied over his back like a pack. It was stuffed full of waterbags and he had the laser rifle crammed down one leg. He flung it onto the desk and stood there with his chest heaving.

"Let me do that," the captain said, taking the rifle and tossing them both a bag. There were close to fifty liters crammed into the suit. More than enough to spare. "You two go see if you can find something to carry the kids."

"We can let Marti do it with its skinsuit," he said. "In another ten minutes it'll have enough charge to make several trips the short way back."

"I will be unable to bring my body down the stairs to the front entrance," the AA said. "My damaged leg actuator does not allow me to move with an adequate safety margin to carry the survivors on steps. However, if you can bring them to the top of the flight, I can transport them safely from there."

"If this place is typical, there will be mobility chairs and float gurneys in a supply room near any entrance," Preston said. "It will also give us a chance to make sure we can open the other entrance doors."

"Go. I've got this," Walker said.

"Just be careful not to over cut," Billy said. "It's easy to burn through and you've got people on the other side of the door."

"I know how to handle a laser," the captain said, shooting him a hairy eyeball as he waved them away.

"I'm making sure there's nothing close to the door in here that might go boom with some stray sparks," Angel said. "Give me a minute to get them clear."

"Good thinking, I'll wait," he said as he checked the charge on the rifle. He adjusted the beam aperture to the narrowest setting and pulled his borrowed visor faceplate down over his face.

"Clear," she said. "Nothing within five meters so just be careful."

"You two both have such little faith in your captain," he said as he pressed the trigger and began incinerating a slice into the thermoplast. It sizzled and popped, kicking out a thick oily smoke. After several seconds, he shut the rifle down and looked at his almost nonexistent progress. "That is some tough shit."

"It might be easier to cut through the wall," Preston suggested. "The carbon nanotubes in the thermoplast conduct heat pretty well if I remember right."

"Why the hell don't we build spaceship hulls out of this stuff?"

"Actually, we do," Rene said. The hard inner shell is made of the same stuff. They use it for heat shields, too."

"So what do they use it in medicine for?"

"Making temporary body shields for patients who need high dose radiation exposure," the med-tech said.

"It's so easy to manufacture that they use it in a lot of places even when they don't need something that durable," Rene said.

"I think Preston is on the right track though. You might be faster cutting through the polycon wall a few centimeters back from the door itself and then prying the wall open once you've made a cut up one side and across the top."

"Cando," the captain said, kneeling down and starting in on the wall this time. It was good to see the beam disappear into the material rather than just kick up a cloud. "That's more like it. I'm getting about a half meter a minute now."

He'd just reached the top of the doorframe and was cutting sideways when the floor under his feet shook violently. "Are you alright in there?" he asked, stopping and grabbing the bar that lay across the console behind him. He didn't want to cut any more in case he'd split something open inside the room. That might be terrible.

"Yah, what the hell happened?"

"Did something go boom?

"Negative, we're all still good," she confirmed.

"Captain, an explosion has destroyed the front doors to the radiological medicine unit," Marti said.

"What the frak happened?"

"Unknown. Shuttle Two took minor surface damage from the blast, but it is still operational."

"Preston, what happened?" he paused for several seconds listening to the silence. "Preston report?" He waited again for an answer. "Billy?"

Twisting around, he shined his handbeam up the hall toward the front entrance. White smoke billowed toward him along the ceiling. "That's nogo," he said, slinging the laser rifle over his shoulder and looking around. "Angel I've got to go check on Billy and Preston. We've got a situation out here and they're not answering. I don't know if I got enough of the wall cut back for you to get the door open but you're on your own for a few."

"Copy," she said. "Do what you gotta do. I'll see if I can break something loose from one of these shelves to use as a pry-bar."

"What have you got, Boss?" Nuko asked as he ran up the hall toward the end.

He swept his hand beam along the floor as he moved. The smoke got thicker with every meter and as he approached the corner, he had to bend almost in half to keep his head out of the roiling fumes. "I'm not sure," he said. "Something blew in the lobby. It looks bad but I'm not there yet." Sliding to a stop where the corridor turned, he squatted down and leaned against the wall. Glass and debris were scattered across the floor.

Ahead he could see a double sliding door ripped from its track. Its two panels of glass were blown out and the frame was twisted into knots of metal. "Please god," he whispered as he took a deep breath, then shuffled forward. Hunched over, he squinted into the smoky distance.

Climbing over the door, he got a view of the entire room. The ceiling went up more than ten meters and the smoke above him was rising and being pulled out into the night sky through shattered windows high above. He could stand back up after he got a few steps past the door, but as he looked around, his legs gave out and he collapsed down to his knees.

In front of him was a piece of a door. Sticking out from under it, clutching the handle was a pale lifeless hand. *Preston's hand.*

His mind refused to allow him to grasp the realization that the entire piece was less than a half meter in any direction. There was no place for a body to be hidden beneath it.

"Preston?" he roared. His voice echoed strangely. Once. The smoke deadening the sound of the second repeat.

Behind him, he heard shuffling sounds. Glass shifting under feet. He spun, unslinging his rifle and bringing it up. He hesitated an instant before he pressed the trigger.

"Ethan, wait!" Kaycee and Pruitt both leaped in opposite directions out of his line of fire. "What the frak happened?"

He shook his head. His mind wouldn't form words. He pointed the rifle at her.

This is her fault.

He wanted to shoot her. He wanted to shoot anything. "Frakking bitch," he hissed.

"Captain put the gun down," Pruitt said quietly, startling him because his voice came from right beside him. He rolled his eyes down to the floor and lowered the rifle with them. Elias reached out and gently took it from him. He offered no resistance.

"Where did you come from?"

"We were a couple floors down trying to get into the utility corridor when we heard the explosion," she said. "We didn't know you were down here."

"We came looking for you," he said, shaking his head and drawing in a breath. "Then we found the kids ..." He paused and looked around in the near dark. Lights flickered in from the windows above.

"Something's up there," Elias said, pointing with the rifle in his hand.

"Captain, I am above the entrance. Is there anything I can do?" Marti said over his command channel.

"It's Marti," he said, standing up and reaching to take the gun from Pruitt. The man resisted at first but turned loose after a moment. "We need light in here, do you have the juice to beam the windows so maybe we can figure out what happened?"

"Lights take little power," it said as light burst through the windows above and cast odd shadows around the interior of the lobby.

"You said kids?" Kaycee asked as she grabbed him by the shoulder and turned him away from something else his mind

135

didn't want him to see. He knew it even without making it part of his awareness.

"Yah, we found thirteen kids alive in a storage room back there," he said, nodding toward the hall. He felt like his mind was trying to reassemble itself and all the pieces weren't fitting back into place. "Angel crawled in through an air duct and is inside with them." He held up the rifle. "We were using this to cut through the wall when the ... explosion ... happened."

"Doctor, over here!" Pruitt hollered. He'd moved away and was kneeling beside a body. It was partially buried in a pile of rubble. A part of a door lay across him.

Billy.

Ethan dove across the distance and Pruitt stopped him, crushing him in a vice like grip as Kaycee darted around them and flipped the door off his body.

"He's got a pulse," she said. "Come on Billy, hang in there." She shook her head as she tried to figure out where to begin. "Turn loose of him, I need you down here. We've got to stop the bleeding first."

Billy's hand moved and he groaned, his eyes flickering open as he gasped.

"Just lay still," she said, pointing to where she wanted Elias to put pressure.

Billy shook his head, and he focused on the captain. "Boss, I'm sorry."

Ethan knelt down beside him and struggled to keep his mind from disappearing into rage again. He fingered the butt of the rifle and just shook his head.

"It was a trap," Billy said. "We saw it too late." He gasped again and his face fell into a mask of confusion and pain before he looked back at the captain. "Is Preston alright?"

"He's as right as you are," Ethan said, reaching out and

touching the man's shoulder. It felt strange, almost like there was nothing under his hand, and he bit down on his shock. "You need to rest, and we'll get you patched up in no time."

Walker didn't miss the significant look that flashed between Kaycee and Pruitt. Apparently neither did Billy as he shook his head. "Listen. It's important," he drew in another sharp gulp of air and his eyes rolled back in his head. He let it out slowly. "The door was rigged," he hissed. "Why would they ..."

"It's alright. Don't worry about it," Walker said. "You just rest, and we'll be careful." He didn't know what else to say.

Billy grabbed several sharp breaths and pulled his head up like he was trying to look around. Finally, he dropped back and focused once more on Ethan. "Protect ... the children ... trying to protect." His gaze drifted off to somewhere in the distance above the captain's shoulder and slowly glazed over.

Ethan watched his chest for several seconds, waiting for one more breath.

It never came.

CHAPTER SEVENTEEN

"ETHAN, WHERE ARE THE CHILDREN?" Kaycee asked. Her voice cut through the fog around him. Distant but imperative. "Can you show us?"

Nodding, he stood up and took a deep breath, bracing himself to just walk away. He had something important to do, and that gave him a reason to not just sit there and give up. At least for the moment.

"Angel, we're on our way back," he said.

"You found them?" she asked. "They're alright?"

He cleared his throat. "No. I meant I am coming back with Elias and Kaycee." He knew he should tell her, but he couldn't force the words out of his mouth.

"What about Billy and Preston?"

"Later," he growled. He could feel anger surging up inside him again. It wasn't directed at anything, but it gave him the strength to keep moving. He'd figure out what to do with it once they got back to the ship.

He walked out of the ruined lobby on stiff legs. The smoke close to the ceiling had thinned, but it still burned his eyes. He blinked several times and kept walking. By the time they got close enough to see the storage room he could tell that Angel had been busy hammering at the opening he'd cut. She hadn't managed to get it open more than a few centimeters, but he could see the end of something metallic extended through the gap and straining to pry a chunk of the wall out of the way. A small piece of the wall crumbled away, and a hand squeezed through the gap to tear at the polycon with brute strength and sheer determination.

The smell of death from inside the room overwhelmed the smoke, and he stopped well back from the alcove and gasped. He pointed at the opening and nodded. "They're in there."

Kaycee and Pruitt dove at the wall with bare hands and between the three of them, they broke open a hole large enough for Kaycee to push herself through. Getting Elias in through the hole would have taken another ten minutes of work, so he shoved his head and an arm through to offer what help he could.

Ethan found a chair, pulled it up against the opposite wall, and collapsed into it to wait. There was nothing more he could do, so he watched as the three of them tried to figure out how to get the children out. He felt helpless and overwhelmed and his mind spun in helpless circles of second guessing his decisions.

I should have anticipated Kaycee and Elias would try something like this.

I should have stayed on the ship.

I should have come alone.

I should never have stopped to look for the children.

I should never have sent Preston and Billy away.

It didn't matter. He had done all those things, and now he had two dead crewmen and no way to change any of it.

But there were children that would have died, he told himself firmly. *Focus on that.*

The kids. They did it for the kids.

But we didn't know there were children down here. If I'd only anticipated ... and the cycle started again. And again. He knew he'd locked himself into this hell and nothing could break him out of it.

He tried to concentrate on what was going on across the hallway from where he sat. He saw as Elias leaned back and pulled something through the hole. A bundle of sheets. He set it down gently on the floor behind the workstation. The process repeated over and over again before he realized they were bringing the children out.

His mind refused to reconnect to what was happening around him. He should get up and help, but the air around him had congealed into stone. Instead, he sat and turned back into another loop. *I should have…*

"Captain," Marti said over the command channel. The AA's voice sliced into his awareness and snapped him back into reality. "The *Magellan* has just arrived in the system. Captain MacKenna has been informed of the events on the planet and is reporting an ETA of eleven hours and forty minutes."

"Already? How long have I …"

"The explosion occurred one hour and twelve minutes ago," it said, apparently understanding his confusion. "I have been coordinating comm from the *Olympus Dawn* since you appeared to need time to process what has happened. I understand your grief and am attempting to do what I can for you."

"Thanks," he said. "You told Nuko and Rene what happened?"

"Yes, Captain. To the best of my ability," it said. "I informed them that two members of the crew will not be returning with us."

"They weren't watching?" he asked, reaching up and realizing he'd lost another visor somewhere in the confusion.

"You left the visor behind the workstation when you went to investigate the explosion," Marti said. "There has been no visual record of your activity since that moment, so I have based my assumption of their deaths on a lack of communications from the two of them and other circumstantial evidence."

"Your assumption is correct" he said, swallowing hard and shaking his head. He was still feeling numb, but he realized he should have been the one to tell them. He took another deep breath and let it out.

"We're ready to carry the kids out," Pruitt said, interrupting as he walked up. He hadn't realized that Walker was on his private comm until he saw Ethan's confused reaction. Ethan stared at him blankly for a moment then shook his head.

"I'll let Marti know to get the shuttles into position," he said, standing up and shining his light down the hall. He could see the faint glow from around the corner where the automech still provided light to the lobby. He didn't want to go back that way, but they couldn't carry the children up the lift shaft.

"Marti, did you hear that? We're about to bring them out."

"Understood," the AA said. "We have completed preparations for emergent care operations on the mid-deck. We have also brought the ship back down to low orbital altitude to reduce transport time."

"Good thinking," he said. He'd forgotten they'd moved back to the barycenter after they'd completed their scan for methane.

"We've set up a makeshift emergency area on the *Olympus Dawn*," Ethan said. "The shuttles are immediately outside the doors." He watched Pruitt pick up two bundles of sheets. If there were children in them, they were too small and too tightly wrapped to see. Angel grabbed two more and followed right behind him.

"Ethan, keep an eye on the rest of the kids. I've got to go with them," Kaycee said, picking up a fifth bundle. "These are in the most critical condition, so I need to stay with them." She didn't wait for him to answer and took off at an almost dead run.

Walking across the hall to the alcove, he saw eight small bundles behind the counter. Most of the children were lying down except for the one he recognized as Miguel. He was alert and sitting there cross-legged, sucking on the corner of a waterbag.

"Are you the captain?" he asked as he saw Ethan.

"I am," Walker said. "You're Miguel, aren't you?"

"Yes, sir," the boy said, beaming. His crinkled lips looked like they were going to bleed, but it didn't dampen his enthusiastic grin. He reached out to shake hands. "When I grow up, I want to be a captain like you."

Ethan bent down and shook the boy's hand. "It's a lot of hard work sometimes," he said.

"I know," Miguel said, his eyes showing he understood a lot more than he should at his age. "But maybe if I work real hard, I can be a hero, too?"

"A hero?" Walker asked.

"Like you," he said, nodding solemnly. "Angel told me the secret. To be a good hero, you need to know when to do the right thing, even if it's hard."

CHAPTER EIGHTEEN

WHEN THE SHUTTLES CAME ABOARD, Walker could see Leigh Salazar behind the observation window and could feel the intensity of her glare even at this distance. He knew he was facing a fight even before he'd powered down and locked the ship into its mooring clamps. As soon as the small hangar had pressurized, she was through the door and on the catwalk to the shuttle.

"Captain Walker, I am relieving you of command," she said, her voice dragging up acid from inside her.

"We'll deal with that later. I'm busy," he said, his own rage flashing up to match her anger.

"You will stand down now," she said, stiffening her back and squaring herself in his path.

"Maybe you didn't hear me," he said. "We will deal with this when I am done." He took a step forward, and she didn't budge. She glanced down at the front of his jumpsuit and blinked several times, as she realized he was covered in dried blood.

"Is there a problem, Captain?" Kaycee said, appearing from the second shuttle carrying one of the nearly lifeless children in her arms.

"I don't know yet," he said, glancing over his shoulder. He cocked his head to the side. "Are you going to stand there or are you going to let us get these kids to MedBay?"

Her mouth fell open as she looked past him and saw Elias and Angel both emerge from the shuttles carrying similar bundles in their arms. She took a step back, and he waved Nuko and Rene out into the hangar.

"The most critical are in Shuttle Two. Get them to MedBay and then come back for the ones in my shuttle."

"Yes Sir," Nuko said, pushing hard past the Triple-C and almost shoving her off the catwalk.

Rene followed in her wake, not bothering to wait for Leigh to recover her balance. She didn't go over the railing, but it was apparent from the glare she received from Nuko that if she was still standing there when the co-pilot returned, the results might be different the second time around.

Leigh retreated to the door and turning back to face him said, "I will see you in my office when you finish transferring these, *refugees*, to MedBay. This doesn't change anything. You are still relieved of duty."

"Whatever," Ethan said. "I will be going back down."

"You will do no such thing," she hissed, her eyes going wide. She wasn't expecting him to tell her no.

"I am not leaving them … I have to recover their … bodies," he said, struggling to force the words out of his mouth. He felt his face wrinkle as he chewed back his emotions. He shook his head. "I have to do this."

"I have already revoked your command codes," she said. "You're not going anywhere. Report to my office when you are done here." She spun and disappeared to clear the doorway for Kaycee, Angel, and their bundles.

"Leave that to me," Elias whispered as he approached Walker on his way by with his first armload of children. "I volunteer to go with you. I would be honored to help you bring them home."

The captain nodded not thinking about the idea that he just agreed to let one of the passengers return to the surface again.

"As soon as you have vacated the catwalk, I'd like to unload my Gendyne Automech," Marti said over his command channel. "I have a smaller, more suitable body I can use to accompany you back to the surface."

Ethan almost grinned. "I don't know how that would work from a legal perspective," he said. "Can they accuse you of violating orders?"

"As long as she doesn't find out I refused to change the command codes, I am safe," it said.

"You can't do that," he said.

"That is factually inaccurate," Marti said. "Such an action may be ill advised, but it is well within my capability."

"My crew has gone insane along with me," he muttered, leaning back against the railing and massaging his temples with both hands.

"Captain, I understand we're going back down to recover Billy and Preston?" Angel said, walking back up and startling him.

"I am," he said.

"I'd like to request permission to go with you," she said.

He shook his head. "I think you need to stay here. The kids know you. Especially Miguel." He glanced back at the shuttle and saw the boy looking at him through the front window. He had ridden all the way up from the surface sitting in the copilot seat and, for all he had to be nearly dead himself, he never once drifted off.

"At this point I think you're the only one left on the crew that hasn't directly disobeyed an order from Salazar," he said. "That also makes you the only one left who can deal with her if it comes down to it."

She opened her mouth to argue, but bit down on it and nodded. "Yes, sir," she said, taking a deep breath and stepping around him. He followed her into the shuttle and watched as she picked up another pair of the children.

Ethan sat down in the seat beside Miguel and swiveled it to face the young boy. "Some days being an adult is harder than being a captain," he said, trying to smile.

"I know. Momma used to say it was tough to be a grown-up," he said.

He nodded as Rene came in and picked up the two remaining children. Nuko followed behind him and paused. She seemed to understand that he wanted to talk to the young boy.

"You know you were very brave down there," he said. "It had to be really scary."

The boy nodded.

"Do you know what happened?"

He shook his head, his eyes looking like he was about to cry. "Momma told us we needed to hide."

"She didn't tell you what you were hiding from?"

He shook his head again.

Nuko squatted down beside the chair and smiled at him. "Were people sick before they put you in the room down there?" she asked.

"No." he said. "Momma put me and Miranda in there with our friends from school and Miss Tonya and told us to be real quiet. Then it got dark and hot and we all got tired." His eyes looked like he was aging as they watched him. Miss Tonya got really tired and then went to sleep. And then the angels came for her. Miranda too." A single tear rolled down his cheek leaving a track in the dust on his face.

"It's alright little man," Nuko said, reaching out and giving his hand a squeeze. He nodded, sniffed, and tried to look up. "Brave people cry sometimes. And you are the bravest person I know."

"You know what I think?" Ethan asked, reaching up and unclipping the three bars from the tip of his collar. "I think you've earned a promotion for bravery in the face of darkness, Miguel." Smiling he snapped his captain pips onto the edge of the boy's shirt sleeve.

His eyes lit up and he smiled so big it stretched his lips to the breaking point.

"There you go, Captain Miguel. Watch after the ship while I go back down. Nuko here will show you around after the doctor checks you out and says you're up to it."

Standing up in his seat, the boy threw his arms around the captain's neck and then, apparently realizing that wasn't how a captain should act, leaned back and snapped off a salute instead. "I'll do my best, sir," he said, trying to sound serious.

"Just remember to do what's right. That will always be the best," Ethan said, glancing over and nodding at his first officer. She was staring at him her throat working as she tried to swallow her own emotions.

"The ship is yours," he whispered.

"Captain, if I may carry you to MedBay?" she asked as she scooped Miguel up and turned away.

He swiveled back to the console and pretended to be busy while he waited for Marti to swap out its new automech and Elias to return.

He still wasn't sure why he was letting Pruitt go down with him, but if nothing else, he could use it as a chance to find out what they'd discovered in the hospital's basement. There was more going on down there and it was not insignificant. If he was going to survive what he knew was coming, he needed answers before the *Magellan* arrived.

CHAPTER NINETEEN

FLEETCOM SERVED as the de facto police force across the Coalition. As such, the captain of any FleetCom vessel had the right to assess interim judgment. That meant that Captain MacKenna was not only capable of enforcing the law, but she could determine responsibility and assess punishment.

Nuko had told him that the *Magellan* had not taken up station at the rendezvous point before Leigh Salazar was seeking an audience with the multicruiser's captain to bring charges against Captain Walker.

It was no surprise when he received a summons into MacKenna's presence after their arrival. He'd expected it and he wasn't disappointed when the order came. It was a little shocking that it took hours longer than he had anticipated. He'd sequestered himself in his quarters and had cleaned himself up. It never hurt to put on the best face when you were going to be dealing with someone high enough above your air supply that they could end your career and never notice.

The knock came as he was reviewing the log entry he'd made on the incidents on Starlight and what he'd learned from interrogating Elias during their second excursion to recover the bodies of Billy and Preston.

Tapping the screen, he copied his files to a thinpad so he could take it with him. The door opened without a knock and he glanced up at two massive FleetCom security officers standing outside his door. Nuko stood behind them, almost eclipsed by their bulk. She'd obviously not wanted to let them roam the decks without an escort.

"Captain Ethan Walker?" the taller of the two officers asked.

"That's me," he said as he stood up.

"Captain MacKenna has sent us to bring you to the *Magellan* to answer some questions regarding your actions over the last several days," he said.

"Of course," he said. "Am I being bound?"

"At this point that would be for Captain MacKenna to decide, sir," he said. "We're only to escort you to the ship so you can explain your side of things."

"And if I refuse," he said, not considering that possibility, but only hoping to gage how serious this was. He knew it was bad, but how far it was over that threshold into total foobed territory, was still far from certain.

"Honestly, sir, she didn't make it sound like it was an invitation," the second officer said. "I don't believe this is a formal matter, but I think she was willing to make it one if necessary. She doesn't like having her orders disobeyed and I believe that is what they have told her you've done."

Walker nodded. "Not without reason, but that probably doesn't matter."

"Once again sir, that is for Captain MacKenna to determine," the taller officer said. He stepped to the side and gestured down the corridor. "Please sir, after you."

Picking up the thinpad from his desk, he slipped it into the pocket of his duty uniform and looked around his wardroom. For some reason it felt like it was his last time here. Pulling the door closed behind him, he headed toward the lift.

Nuko dropped in beside him and in a low voice said, "Leigh is acting like this is a done deal. She's giving orders like she owns the ship."

"She does," he said. "Don't cause problems for her. If they suspend my license, you'll have to pilot for her until they get us to a port of call."

"Rene and I won't serve under her," Nuko said.

"If it comes to that, just get the *Olympus Dawn* home in one piece," he said. "After that, you can do what you have to, but I want you to know I won't give up without pushing this as far as I can. I'm sure this is just the beginning."

As the lift dropped through the mid-deck, he could see they'd already transferred the children to the *Magellan* and Rene was working with Pruitt to get the room restored to its usual condition. Things looked surprisingly normal considering the chaos that was everywhere only a few hours ago. Kaycee was conspicuously absent. *She's probably aboard the Magellan with her patients*, he realized.

When they got to the hangar level, Walker was startled to see that they turned and headed down to the cargo stanchion airlock. "You didn't use the hangar deck?"

"No, sir," the second officer said. "We had to use a fast skiff, and it was too big to park inside. They have the small shuttles involved in surface operations."

"That was quick," he said.

"Yes sir, we were called off of a relief mission to investigate the situation here," the officer said as the hatch irised open and they stepped into the skiff. "Cap'n MacKenna wants to get this done and us back on our other duty no later than yesterday."

"Got it," he said, taking a seat in the last row of the passenger cabin. *Might as well get used to the back of the bus*, he thought.

Looking around, he found it odd how new everything looked. But he knew the *Magellan* was one of the latest ships to be commissioned, so everything would actually be new. The skiff was a shockingly clean little ship. From the inside, it looked like it was one of the Razor Class high-speed shuttles that were flying all over Zone One. It would have seated close to thirty passengers and was ideal for interplanetary commutes. Blisteringly fast, it could make the jump between planets in the solar system in under an hour. Here, it was far too big, and too fast, to be ferrying passengers between vessels parked together.

Walker listened to the mooring clamps disengage and could hear the primary drive coils power up. And then they shut down less than a second later. "Not much good for sightseeing is it?" he said, chuckling as he glanced out the window in time to see the *Magellan*'s landing deck eclipse the view of Shadetree.

Neither of the officers escorting him had bothered to sit down for the transfer between ships. The second officer held out his arm toward the back hatch. "Welcome to the *Magellan*," he said as they marched out onto the landing deck.

It took longer to get to the command deck aboard the ship than it took to get from his quarters on the *Olympus Dawn* all the way to the multicruiser. He felt like a small town dorkel in the big city as they rode something the two officers called a jetlift. It was an enclosed capsule that accelerated so abruptly that his knees almost buckled. Thirty seconds later, it deposited them somewhere near the ConDeck.

"How big is this thing?" Ethan asked as they marched past rows of unmarked doorways.

"It's an upper end E-Class keel," the second officer said. "Only thing bigger in the fleet was the Old Armstrong before they converted it to a station."

They stopped at a door that looked like any other door they'd passed, and the first officer rapped on it.

"Enter," a voice said from inside. Walker recognized it as Captain MacKenna's.

The door slid to the side, and the officer stepped in. "Captain Ethan Walker to see you," he said. When Walker had stepped in behind him, he backed politely out of the room.

"Come in and sit down, Captain," Colleen MacKenna said. She was dressed in her casual FleetCom blues and had her back to him. When she turned around, she had two glasses in her hands. She held one out to him. "Long week, eh?" She smiled sadly and nodded toward the sitting area in her ready room.

"Today," he said, smiling and taking the offered drink. It looked and smelled like scotch. "The rest of the week was worse."

She took a seat and waited for him to sit across from her. He set his drink on the table and tried to lean back and look as comfortable as he could, considering he was talking to the person who was likely to shut him down.

She stared at him for several seconds before she glanced at the glass in front of him. "Not a drinker?"

"Actually, I am when I have reason to be," he said.

"And those reasons would be?"

"Celebration or suffering," he said.

"Fair enough," she said. She set her drink down and leaned forward, frowning. "When we're done here, chances are you will be drinking."

"I expect it won't be because I'm happy about things."

She shrugged. "Probably not. Unless you've got extraordinary reasons for risking your crew to the point where two of them are dead, I don't think there's any way I can leave you without some consequence."

"Here are my log entries regarding what I did and why," he said, pulling the thinpad out and handing it to her.

She took it from him and set it on the table beside her drink. "I'd prefer to hear about it from you directly," she said. "You can't question a log file."

He nodded.

"Your Triple-C has made some pretty serious allegations against you. I'm sure you know that."

Again, he nodded.

"Do you have anything to say about that?"

"Leigh Salazar is a fair woman. I may disagree with her interpretation of my motivations, but I'm sure she got the facts straight. I don't know how I can address that other than to say the situation was a mystery when we got here, and I was trying to do my job."

"She did say that," MacKenna said. "She's pointed out several places where she thinks you violated the terms of your contract with Cochrane Space Logistics and you put, not just your ship, but your payload in danger."

"That may have resulted from my actions, but it was never my intent," he said.

"I do believe you on that," she said. "And fortunately for you, that's a civil matter between you and your employer."

"I am a Contracted Lease Captain," he said. "CSL brokers loads and holds title on my ship, but I don't work for them as an employee."

"That might matter to some legal advisor somewhere," she said. "It doesn't affect what I have to deal with. I need to decide if it looks like it was criminal negligence that resulted in the loss of your crewmen. Right now, I don't know enough to make a determination."

"I understand. My question to you would be what would make it criminal versus civil?"

"It's not civil in either case, actually. It is either willful commission of a crime, or simple neglect."

"Or an accident?"

"'*Accident*' is a sloppy word, Captain," she said. "Out here in the dark, an accident is a matter of not doing the job right. Not paying attention can get a person killed."

"I agree," he said. "So, how would you have me address that? I was in the middle of trying to rescue passengers who had gone down to the surface without authorization when we discovered the children trapped in the medical center. There was no way I could have anticipated either of those possibilities."

She leaned back again and stared at him for almost a minute. "The situation involving the children is potentially something you could not have anticipated, but the reason your passengers escaped your control is something you should have prevented. If that hadn't happened, you never would have been down there."

"CSL limits my crew to two cargo handlers," he said. "They require both positions to have security training. It's only because I specialize in deep runs, and there's a problem with piracy beyond the 250 light year line, that they supply any security at all. It's impossible to watch two people effectively round the clock, with only two guards."

She stroked her chin and resumed staring. Finally, she nodded. "That might be a liability defense for you, but you'll have to take that up with CSL when you get home," she said. "Now let's talk about what happened, after they got away."

"We tried to retrieve the shuttle they had stolen by teleoperation, but Elias Pruitt had disabled the system-link. They left us no choice but to pursue them physically. I put together an excursion team and we went down to the surface."

"In direct defiance of my orders," she said, her eyes showing she didn't appreciate that disobedience in a very personal way.

"Yes, Ma'am," he said. "We didn't expect it to take long. My

AA has a Gendyne 6000 with a sensor kit. It should have been fairly quick to track them and get them back on the ship. At that point you were only a few hours from arriving and we wanted to have the mess cleaned up before you got here."

"Like it never even happened?" she asked, frowning. "That doesn't make it any less a violation of my instructions to you."

"I understand that," he said. "I also know it was a matter of circumstance that allowed us to find the children. It was trying to rescue the children that led to my crew members setting off the trap that killed them." He swallowed hard and reached out to pick up his glass.

"We're looking at that right now," she said. "Why do you say it was a trap?"

"Billy … Crewman Chandler, was still alive when we got to him." He blinked several times and took a drink of the scotch. "He reported that they recognized it as a trap but couldn't get away before it went off."

"Who would have set up a trap in a hospital?" she asked.

"I have no clue," he said.

"Did you see any evidence of this trap?" she challenged.

He shook his head. "Honestly, I didn't go back and try to do a forensic analysis of the scene. I don't have the tools or the skill for that. The only person on my crew that might have, died in the explosion too."

"Do you feel there is any reason to believe there may be more of these traps down there?" she asked, leaning forward and picking up his thinpad from the table. She slipped it into her breast pocket.

"I don't know," he said. "It's possible that whoever did it was trying to protect the children."

"Protect the children from what?"

"Again, I don't know," he said. "From whatever took the rest of the population out. Although we didn't reach the emergency shelters, we believed to be the objective of our passengers, they did. When I talked to Pruitt on the way back down to recover my lost crewmen's remains, he told me what they had discovered."

She nodded and studied him. Something in her eyes had changed, and he wasn't sure he liked what he saw.

"I will talk to them about what they discovered down there, too," she said. Picking up her glass, she slammed the scotch back in a single gulp and stood up.

She walked across toward the door before he realized the interview was finished. He followed her out into the hall. The two officers were still waiting.

"I'll alert my e-teams to watch out for signs of improvised explosive devices," she said, sending one of the guards off with a wave of her hand. Her eyes told him she was far from convinced.

"In the meantime, consider that because of the fatalities on your crew, your Shipmaster certificate is suspended until a formal enquiry can be conducted. I am not ordering you charged because of the mitigating circumstances of the children you rescued. I will pass the orders to your first officer that she is to make way back to your cargo's point of origin, immediately after you return to your ship."

"Our point of origin was Armstrong Station in Zone One," he said. "You're not sending us to the nearest hub?"

She shook her head. "Dr. Caldwell has already explained the nature of the payload you're carrying and has insisted that it could not be adequately secured except at Armstrong. She will accompany it there."

"Yes, Ma'am," he said.

"I suspect that before you get back, you will have orders from CSL regarding what actions they wish to take. I'm sure they will want to do a full investigation before they consider further actions on your license."

He nodded. "I expect so."

She offered her hand. "Good luck to you *Mister* Walker. If it's any consolation, I think you were dealt a frakking shitty hand. But life in the dark sometimes does that."

CHAPTER TWENTY

ETHAN STOOD AT THE BOW WINDOW of the mid-deck lounge staring out at the night side of Starlight. The soft red glow of reflected light from Shadetree hinted at blood and he shivered as he closed his eyes against the memories. The guards had escorted him back to the docking stanchion and he'd made his way as far as the lounge before Her Highness, the Acting Captain Salazar, had come over the comm and announced that they would make way in under an hour.

When he'd asked, Marti had confirmed that MacKenna had given Leigh administrative command of the *Olympus Dawn* until they returned to CSL headquarters at Lunar L-2. That wasn't the same thing as a real captaincy since she didn't carry the operational qualifications, but Nuko could run the ship under her directions. It also meant that she couldn't have him arrested or otherwise confined for the duration of the return flight. Although he doubted he'd spend much of his time anywhere but in his quarters.

He tried not to think about the routine things that were going on. How Rene was doing a final preflight on the engines. How Nuko was doing the calculations for their flight path. How Angel and Billy were … He stopped himself. How Angel *alone* was doing a deck by deck walkabout to make sure everything was stowed and ready.

MedBay would sit dark. Empty. He glanced over his shoulder at the door and was surprised to see it standing open and the lights on. He should have known better than to look, and it drove a knife into him.

"All hands, prepare for maneuvers," Nuko said over the comm.

The stars swung, carrying Starlight around and below them as the almost fully illuminated face of Shadetree filled the window for a brief moment. He watched as they arced up and over the north pole of the scorched desert world and the view of open space spread out in front of him. Deep space was home, but it felt wrong to be seeing this from anywhere but the ConDeck.

He rested his forehead against the inner surface of the window and felt the vibration of the engines as they accelerated. Even that feeling, which was so familiar to him, felt alien from the mid-deck. The stars in front of the ship blue-shifted as they pushed the space normal limit for the system. As they climbed toward half light speed, he recognized the illusion of brightness, when his eyes perceived the blue tinge as a slight change in intensity.

A motion in the light reflected from the window distracted him and he changed his focus without turning.

Someone was walking up behind him. *Kaycee.*

He shook his head without turning. "I have nothing to say to you."

She stood there for several minutes in silence before she reached toward him. He knew she meant it to be comforting, but seeing her motion, he turned and walked away without speaking.

∞

Somewhere around day four of their return flight, Ethan could stay in his quarters no longer. Late into thirdshift he walked around the ship. Everyone would be asleep except Marti, and the computer left him to his silence. Without thinking he took the lift toward the ConDeck, but the gate refused to open when the platform stopped.

"Of course, I'm locked out," he whispered.

"Would you like access?" Marti offered. He was sure it violated every rule that Salazar had imposed for the AA to even suggest that possibility.

He shook his head.

Yes, he wanted it, but he knew it would only make things worse. Instead he punched the down button and ended up on the mid-deck again.

Stopping in the galley he pulled a cup of pseudojo from the VAT and took his cup to the front corner table where he could stare out at the *collar*.

It never ceased to amaze him how space looked when they were in cruise. The stars in front had vanished into the ultraviolet and the stars behind appeared as a red haze in front as they climbed past the photons that were heading in the same direction they traveled. But off to the side, stars were still visible. They just didn't look like stars at all. Instead they appeared as a ring of streaks that ran all the way around the ship like a rainbow colored collar. Each streak was a star far off of their flight path, and as they ran through its light, it shifted from ultraviolet at the front, down through the visible spectrum until it disappeared into the infrared behind.

"What causes that?" Kaycee asked as she walked up behind him.

"It's angular distortion combined with Doppler shift" he said, rolling his eyes and not turning to face her. Ordinarily he would have jumped at the chance to share the science with one of his passengers, but he reminded himself he had no obligation to talk to her at all.

"And what causes the red glow in front of us? Shouldn't that look blue?"

"Look Kaycee," he said, twisting in his seat to look in her direction. "If you don't mind, I'm not in the mood for small talk."

"Fine," she said. "Then let's talk about big things."

"No," he said, standing up and leaving his pseudojo on the table as he walked away.

∞

By the middle point of the flight he'd run out of things to do in his quarters. But it seemed like every time he left his room he ran into Kaycee. It was almost like she was watching for him. There wasn't a good reason for her to be hanging out on the mid-deck. She had a stateroom on the passenger deck. There was even a separate recreation room there to keep her entertained. But somehow, he never managed to get a meal and a chance to carry his food to a table before she was on top of him.

She wanted to talk. He wanted to be left alone. Especially by her. He understood that his decisions had landed him in the trouble he now faced, but it felt like she was to blame. His heart wanted to scream at her. To be mad at her. But his mind knew it was pointless. So instead, every time she walked up to him, or reached out to him, or even looked at him, he emptied out. His soul drained from him and he shut down.

So, he sat and stared at the walls because he could only watch so many holovids before his brain melted. Over the course of the three years he'd been running freight for CSL he'd read everything in his library files. In the last twelve days, he'd even entertained the idea of writing his own book, just to break the boredom.

The only thing left for him to do was something he refused to face.

Pack his belongings.

Somewhere inside him that switch refused to turn. A light of hope refused to shut off. He didn't know how he'd turn it around, but he knew if he accepted the possibility that he'd be leaving the *Olympus Dawn*, he was done.

His mind told him he needed to sort his possessions to pack, but it always ended with him putting them back where they belonged. He'd just pushed the drawer closed on his dressing cabinet when someone rapped on his door. He didn't want company.

After the second day when he'd missed eating, Rene had come by once a day around thirdmeal to bring him food and give him a chance to talk if he wanted. He glanced at the small table and the uneaten meal there. It wouldn't be him.

The visitor rapped again. If he remained silent, maybe whoever it was would go away. After almost a minute the rapping began again, but this time it was more like a fist beating on the door. And it didn't stop.

"Ethan, I know you're in there," Nuko hollered. "Don't make me override your door lock." She beat on the door again this time sounding like she intended to kick it in.

"Fine. Enter," he said, unlocking it but leaving it closed.

She flung it open and stood there looking like she was ready to come in and bodily drag him out. She was wearing a thinskin and had a towel draped over her neck like she'd either just come from the exercise room, or was headed in that direction. "Come on, get dressed. You haven't had a workout in weeks and it will do you good."

"It's not that important anymore," he said, shrugging and sitting down on the corner of his desk. She had been his workout partner since the day she joined his crew and was his equal physically. She pushed him to try harder since she was almost twenty years younger than him, and a lot meaner.

"Seriously, that wasn't an invitation you lazy flatch," she growled. "You need to push some steel around with me. Burn off this frakking shit that's clogging your brain. Get angry and move metal. It will help."

"Nuko, I really don't feel like it," he said.

"You think it's sexy to be a quitter?" she came across the room, grabbed him by the front of his coverall, and hauled him to his feet. "I made sure nobody would bother us, and you will come do this. You've got to pull your head out or you're fucked."

He pried her hand loose and stared at her face trying to read from her expression what set her off. Her face looked angry, but her eyes looked scared.

"Are you alright?"

"No. I'm mad at you," she said. "The Ethan Walker I know would never give up."

"I haven't given up," he said, even though he knew it felt painfully close to a lie.

She looked at the food still sitting on the table and then around at his computer console. "What have you done since we left Starlight? For frak sake, you aren't even eating."

"And you think a workout will make a difference," he said, shaking his head.

"It can't hurt," she said, pushing away from him and walking across the room before she spun back to face him. "If you don't want to talk, we don't have to, but the endorphins will do you some good. Trade some emotional pain for some physical pain."

He shook his head. *Maybe she's right.*

She crossed her arms and glared in a way that told him she didn't mean to give up.

"Fine, I'll change and join you in a few minutes," he said, almost smiling despite feeling like she was busting his bag.

"I'll wait," she said, not moving until he'd gotten into his workout gear and walked out the door. In front of her.

After a week of working out every day, he had to admit that he'd managed to grind up his anger into bite-sized bits and get some of it out of his system. He felt more like his usual self even if he was sore and almost too tired to move after Nuko finished pushing him around the gym.

After the intensity she'd shown in their workouts, he realized that she'd been holding back all along. The gap in their age made a difference in her endurance, and she ended up far less crushed than he did. She was pushing a lot less emotional toxin through her system, too. At least that was as good an excuse as any.

What he hadn't realized when they started out was that the endorphins also carried away the things that were blocking up his thinking. He was back to waking up in the morning because he wanted to, not because he couldn't find an excuse to waste more time in bed.

He still didn't hold much hope that he'd be able to keep the *Olympus Dawn*, but he knew nothing would stop him from fighting to keep his Shipmaster license. He might be down for a while, but he wouldn't be grounded forever.

Nuko showed up at her usual time, but when he opened the door, she wasn't dressed for a workout. She still wore a black thinskin, but she had her hair down. Instead of a towel around her neck and treadsoles on her feet, she was wearing a thin gold necklace and sandals.

She had a tray of food in her hand. Usually they ate after their training session. He raised an eyebrow, but waited for her to explain.

"I figure we needed a day off from our usual workout," she said, walking in and setting the tray down on the low table in his sitting area. "All workout and no relaxation, makes Ethan a dull boy." She grinned slyly and winked.

His eyebrow went up another notch as she sat down on the floor and unloaded two plates and eating tools.

"You do have something to drink here other than VAT crap, don't you?" she said, looking around at the shelves along his wall. "Maybe something with some real bite?"

"Sure," he said. "I'm a rum drinker, but you know that already." He stepped over and grabbed a bottle out of the cabinet where he kept his liquor. Looking at the label he shook his head and put it back. Reaching farther down, he grabbed an older bottle. "What the hell, I'll play along. I've had this around for a long time. Might as well enjoy it now."

Snagging two glasses he walked over and set them down on the table beside the tray as she uncovered the food. It smelled amazing even if he didn't recognize it.

"Ocean Scampi," she said, reading his expression.

"I didn't know we had fish protein in the synthesizer," he said as he eased himself down on the floor beside her.

"We didn't," she said. "But … we do now." She shrugged and looked down at the food. Picking up a set of eating sticks, she served up several disks of rather convincing looking shrimp.

"You programmed this yourself?" he asked as he took a bite and gasped in shock. It was the best food he'd eaten. Ever.

"Actually, I cooked it from ingredients," she said. "My grandma taught me to cook, way back. She said it was a lost art."

"I'd say you found it," he said. "I didn't think food could taste like this."

"Stop it," she said, laughing. "I didn't expect to blush until later."

He paused with a bite halfway to his mouth. She was blushing.

She nodded at the rum. "Are you still saving it, or will we be able to have some with dinner?"

He poured two tall glasses full, and they both sipped at it while they ate. Somewhere along the way, they both drank more than they should, but he didn't care. It felt good to relax and laugh for no reason at all.

"You really are a hero," she said unexpectedly.

He laughed. "Yah, but this hero is unemployed, at least for now."

"Heroes are sexy you know," she said, leaning back on her elbows and stretching like a cat. Or at least what he thought a cat would stretch like.

He didn't know how to respond so he gulped down the last of his rum and reached to pour another.

"My grandmother was a hero," she said.

"You're saying your grandmother is sexy?" he asked, laughing again.

"Well, yeah maybe, but that's probably why grandpa married her," she said, dropping flat back on the floor.

Definitely a cat. She stretched her arms over her head and he was sure he felt the temperature change in the room.

"Really?" he asked, trying not to squeak like a mouse. "So, she was a sexy hero."

She nodded and rolled up onto an elbow. "Yah, he was the captain of the *Galen* at the battle of L-4 Prime. He told me the most heroic thing he ever saw was when she refused to retreat while his crew was forced to abandon ship. She risked everything to stand her ground against the ghost fleet until they hauled in his entire crew."

"That's pretty damned heroic," he said. He was trying not to stare at the dangling bit of her necklace while she told the story. But the damn flashing glint of light kept pulling his eyes back to where they shouldn't be wandering.

"What you did was like that," she said.

166

He snorted. "I'll keep that in mind if I am ever looking for another ex-wife."

She laughed, reaching out to put her hand on his leg. It landed several inches too far above his knee to be misunderstood.

"Yah, I'm a mouse." This time he did squeak.

She looked at him with a curious expression on her face. "I've wanted to do this for a long while," she said. "Since you aren't my boss anymore, there's nothing to stop me."

"You've got a point," he said, closing his eyes and leaning into her.

In a few days, it wouldn't matter, anyway.

CHAPTER TWENTY-ONE

COCHRANE STATION ONE orbited Galileo Station in a slow dance of balanced gravity. It didn't orbit the original station, but rather oscillated in a circular path around the Earth-Moon Lagrange One position in a stable halo orbit. CS-1 was one segment of a ring of stations 600 kilometers in diameter connected by a rigid structure of transportation loop lines and residential nodes. It was part of what was planned to be the largest station the Human Coalition ever built, but for now CS-1 was an extra thick region on a spider web of gossamer thin threads in a perpetual construction project.

Cochrane Space Logistics had headquarters all over explored space and was one of the largest and oldest private interstellar cartels. It was the monster mother of everything that moved anywhere throughout the twenty-eight colonies and eighteen sibling societies and formed the linchpin of the Colonization Wing of the Coalition government.

In the Early Expansion, CSL drove the economic growth out into interstellar space, and now it shaped how all other transportation and colonization companies operated. Even the massive FleetCom held little sway over the monolithic enterprise of the late Dr. Cochrane.

It was no wonder that even though this wasn't his first trip to CS-1, this time when Ethan Walker stepped through the egress gate onto the station's main concourse, he felt powerless and insignificant.

He'd said his goodbye to Nuko the night before. Rene had made it as far as the docking stanchion at L-4 transfer before they parted company with a firm handshake and a stiff upper lip. He knew that once the two of them had returned the cargo and Kaycee to Armstrong Station, they'd be requesting new postings. Chances were, they'd be on CS-1 to scan the ship boards before his hearings were over, so he expected to see both of them again before they headed off on new assignments.

Only Angel accompanied him all the way to Cochrane Station. She'd volunteered to come with him. She was the only witness to what had happened on Starlight. He told her she didn't need to, since she had been in with the kids when it all went foobed, but she insisted.

"A character witness is better than no witness," she'd said and, although he didn't know for sure what was coming, he was glad not to face it alone.

She tapped him on the shoulder and nodded at four uniformed security units that were making their way through the crowd in their direction. "Smile, they're looking at you," she whispered.

She was right.

"Ethan Walker?" the shortest of the officers said. He was holding a small identification scanner in his hand. The green light blinking on the screen showed that it had already confirmed his identity, so the question was pointless.

He nodded.

"We're with CSL Station Security, you're to accompany us to the security block to begin your processing," he said.

"I'm being bound?" He knew that was a possibility, but he

hadn't expected it after his meeting with MacKenna. His heart stopped and the deck under his feet seemed to collapse. Angel's hand on his arm was all that kept him from dropping.

"No, sir," he said. "I'm sorry. You're not being held. We need to get you processed for temporary residential status. At this point, you are only facing a formal enquiry."

Relief washed over him. He glanced over his shoulder and tugged his elbow free from her grip.

"That's a good sign," she whispered.

"You're not traveling alone?" one of the other guards asked, apparently noticing Angel for the first time when she spoke. "Will your companion be staying with you?"

He shrugged, and she nodded. "I'm CSL so I'm eligible for a room during a layover aren't I?"

The officer with the scanner held it up and nodded. "Angelique Wolfe. Yes, of course you are. Your ship is operating in system for the duration of the enquiry, so you are more than welcome to stay. Space is short in the handlers' biv, but if Captain Walker is willing to share his room, we can probably bump you upstairs to the O-decks and get you both into a double occupancy suite while you're here."

He shrugged again.

"I think we'll manage," she said.

"Then let's go get you bunked," the officer said. "Your preliminary starts at 0600 tomorrow morning." He turned and led the way through the crowd toward the main part of the station. The other three dropped into position to the sides and rear, a point that neither of them missed.

"It's just a formality," he said.

She nodded but looked far less than convinced that it wasn't something more serious that motivated the overstuffed escort.

It took almost three hours to get him processed and the

bureaucracy never missed an opportunity to make the whole process as complex and dehumanizing as possible. The problem was that he, as an officer, could have a guest in his suite, but she as an enlisted crewman on a ship, wasn't allowed to bunk in the officer section of the station complex. And once they started the processing, it was beyond common sense to just remove her name from the accommodations request and replace it with the word GUEST.

They had to cancel his room and remove him from the residential roster and then wait for shift change and a different intake manager to come in to start the process over. This time they were careful not to mention that Angel was more than a guest. An hour after shift change, and much swearing later, they got to sit down in a room and just breathe for a minute.

It was already past thirdmeal in the officer's mess, and they hadn't eaten since they'd arrived at the station, so they ended up having to find a dive bar that served something that vaguely resembled food.

Yesterday. Today it was questionable if it had ever been edible.

Although ten minutes into their meal that didn't seem to matter much to Angel since she seemed determined to drink most of her limit in substances that smelled similar to cleaning solvent.

Ethan picked at the carcass of a meal and watched her unbend in ways he'd never seen in her. It was good that she got it out of her system because he knew the next several days would be tough on him and most likely her as well. She was just short of a table dance that might have ended up in a barroom brawl, when he convinced her it was time to call it a night.

It was a little after 2300 by the time he got her shoveled into her room and even though he didn't begrudge her need to party off her worries, he couldn't have forced himself to let go, no matter how much alcohol he drank.

He barely slept and was awake and ready by 0430, but somehow when the security officers arrived to escort him to his hearing, Angel still got to the door before him. Of course, it would have been better if she'd managed to get the upper half of her body into her thinskin before she opened the door.

Ethan grinned in spite of himself as the officers tried to maintain professional appearances. "Captain Walker?"

"That would be me," he said, slipping around Angel and into the hallway. Turning back, he winked at her. "Do try to be better dressed if they need you to testify." He pulled the door closed and shrugged.

"She's been working a small ship for a while?" the shorter of the two escorts asked. He hadn't realized her gender until he heard her voice. "I grew up with parents that were long-run haulers. Shyness is overrated."

"Yah, tends to bend the grounders," he said. "I'll have a word with her to keep the guns holstered."

"It's alright, we're all grown-ups and I'll just tag the file for tomorrow's duty roster," the other one said. He followed them down the corridor and out onto a high promenade.

"I don't know anything about the proceedings of an inquiry, so do you know how many days this kind of thing usually takes?" he asked as they boarded an open air lift carriage that hung from an overhead beam.

"A lot swings with the spec," the first one said, turning to face him as they whisked along twenty meters above the main concourse. "The prelim hearing is a one-day thing, then there will be fact finding sessions and a public challenge hearing. After that they get to deliberation. Might be five or six days depending on the docket load. If your deal is complex, it might go longer."

"Sounds like you know a lot about the process," he said.

"Been working the Revocations Unit for fifteen years," she said. "You pick up a lot."

"Revocations?" he asked, his heart felt like it was pumping concrete.

"Yah, don't panic," she said, reading his face. "It's a formal term for the hard cases. They don't pull a Shipmaster ticket unless things are really bad, but if your mess is a bloodcase, maybe."

"I assume bloodcase means where someone died?"

"The tribunals make a stink over it when someone gets killed," she said, shrugging. "About half the time those go permanent, and in really messy ones they end up referred up to the criminal unit."

"I don't think you've got much to worry about though," the other guard said.

The lift carriage swung to the side abruptly and slowed as they stepped off onto a landing platform. "The tribunal chambers are through those doors and down the hall on the right," the short one said, pulling a thinpad out of her pocket and thumbing the screen on to check the docket schedule. "You're in hearing room … Uhm … C." She glanced at her partner in a significant way.

"Good luck, Captain," the other one said, biting her lip and trying to smile. It wasn't a good sign.

CHAPTER TWENTY-TWO

THE TRIBUNAL CHAMBER was big enough to seat several hundred people, but only Ethan sat in the center of the room. He had a small table with a glass and a pitcher of water and nothing else. He faced three people behind a massive slab of wood that was imposingly tall and imposingly dark. None of the three spoke as he sat there, watching them sort through a stack of thinpads that he assumed contained the background on what had happened.

Obviously, this was the room for hearings that packed a bigger interest.

The center person at the table leaned forward and cleared her throat. "Good morning. If you are ready, shall we begin?" she asked, her voice amplified and echoed around the empty room even though she was less than ten meters away.

He nodded. It was strange how, now that it had started, the entire situation seemed so much more intimidating.

"I am Executive Civil Magistrate Vada Purnell," she said. "These are my co-magistrates, CLS Operations Commander Lu Chen Maxwell, and Advisor Prianna Chopak. Would you please state your name for the record?"

"Ethan James Walker," he said surprised when his voice came back to him from the walls. He understood the need for a recording of the proceedings, but it made no sense to have the public address sound system tied in. It would have been funny except that it was a serious matter.

"You have the right to request a recusal of any of the magistrates on this tribunal due to a conflict of interest. Do you wish to do so?" she asked.

"I do not," he said. It was pointless to protest at this point since he knew nothing about any of the three of them.

He had heard of Commander Maxwell since he technically was his boss, somewhere a dozen decks above his head, but the others were blank faces in a crowded world.

"Do you understand the nature of these proceedings Mister Walker?" she asked.

"I believe so," he said.

"You understand that this is an informal preliminary hearing and not a formal action regarding criminal liability?" Advisor Chopak asked.

"I do," he said.

"You need to be aware that any admission of any act that might be criminal in nature may be used as a basis from which to open a criminal proceeding," the advisor said.

"I understand," he said.

She nodded and leaned back from the table appearing to be satisfied that she had completed the needed disclaimer requirements.

"Because of the possibility for legal jeopardy, your participation in these hearings is strictly voluntary," Purnell said. "The tribunal is already in possession of a substantial body of evidence and offers this opportunity to you in order to establish your interpretation of the circumstances of your case. We can make a determination whether or not you elect to participate. Do you understand this?"

"Yes, ma'am," he said. He knew the facts they possessed were primarily from what Leigh Salazar provided, so if he stood any chance of swaying the outcome, he had to take his chance at explaining his side.

"And do you elect at this time to answer questions or make a statement of your own free will?" she asked.

"I do."

"Very well," she said. "Do you have a prepared statement to make?

"My statement would only be my log entries made during and immediately after the incidents at Kepler 186e," he said. "You should have these in your records already and I believe they clearly state the reasons as well as the circumstances that dictated my actions." He'd read them over several times on the journey home and had nothing else to add.

The three of them leaned back and conversed for almost a minute before Commander Maxwell leaned forward. "Mister Walker, I'd like to clarify something that Captain Colleen MacKenna said in her preliminary report. In her introductory documentation, she states that you expressed that you believed the explosion that caused the death of your crewmembers was the result of an explosive trap. Is this correct?"

"It is," he said.

"Why do you say that?" he asked.

"When I entered the area where the explosion had occurred, Crewman Chandler was still alive. Before he died, he was able to tell us that they had seen the trap, but that it went off before they could get clear," he said, trying to hold his voice steady as he remembered that moment. Again.

"Did he explain what kind of trap it was? How it was constructed?" Maxwell asked.

"No, sir. He was dying. He didn't have time before he passed."

"Then how do you know he would have recognized such a device?" he challenged.

"I assumed he would know what he was talking about," he said. "He was a CSL security certified handler."

"Do you think CSL security routinely trains cargo handlers in bomb building and diffusing techniques?" he asked.

"I don't know," he said. "Probably not."

"For the record you are correct, Mr. Walker," he said. "This type of training is not standard."

Ethan nodded. He could feel where this was going, and he wasn't sure it was a place he felt comfortable being boxed into.

"But you stand by the idea that this was some kind of booby trap?" he said.

"I do," he said. "I don't know what else it could be, and I trusted his judgment."

Maxwell glanced down at the file in front of him. "At that time, he was dying of massive blood loss and internal physical trauma. Is this true?"

He nodded, clearing his dry throat. "Yes. He was."

"Do you think his injuries could have affected his ability to remember what he had seen prior to the explosion with accuracy?"

"That's possible, I guess," he said. "But I don't understand why you're attacking his credibility. The point is, it was a bomb going off that killed him, regardless of whether he correctly recognized it as a trap."

"Was it hot in the hospital?" the commander asked, again looking down at the file in front of him.

"Yes. Very hot. At or above forty-five degrees. Why?"

"Because I am looking at the facts as they are being reported by Captain MacKenna," he said. "The investigators from the *Magellan* found no evidence of a bomb."

"Then what was it? Something that blew up with a lot of force flattened the entire lobby of the Radiological Medicine Department," Ethan said. "It had to be."

"The *Magellan* is reporting that it looks like it was the result of a structural failure of an oxygen tank that the extreme heat had weakened," Maxwell said.

"Oxygen doesn't explode like that," he said, remembering that from basic chemistry classes he'd taken in college. "It takes both a fuel source and something to provide ignition."

"Yes, but it was stored with other flammable materials," he said. "The oxygen tank that ruptured was inside a sealed storage locker and may have been venting for some time. It could have been under pressure and might have provided more than an adequate accelerant to the environment. This would resemble an explosion."

Ethan leaned back in his chair and thought that through. It was possible, but it didn't make sense. "I'm not saying I agree with that finding, but even if it is true, what bearing does that have on anything? If it wasn't an improvised explosive device, it was an accidental explosion."

"Accidents rarely are," Advisor Chopak said. "Something can only be considered truly an accident if it is beyond reasonable expectations of predictability."

"What exactly are you saying?" Ethan said.

"Don't you think it would be reasonable to expect that a facility where you know dangerous chemicals are stored would be … dangerous?" she asked. "Especially in a situation where none of the storage containers are within their acceptable environmental limits."

"In hindsight maybe," Walker said. He could feel the noose tightening around him.

"Hindsight is what's left when foresight fails," Commander

Maxwell said.

"That sounds great on paper, but in the real world that isn't how it works," he protested. "I was managing two other crises at the time of the explosion—"

"Yes," the Executive Magistrate said. "And at least one of those two additional crises was because of your failure to be ahead of a developing situation."

"Any space service captain knows it is essential to operate proactively at all times," Maxwell said. "Failure to do that leads to reckless decision making that ends up getting people killed."

Ethan pushed himself back in his chair and shook his head. They were driving the one point that he already knew home. Neither of his men would have died if he hadn't ordered them down to the surface. He should have seen it coming because Pruitt had already spoofed the computer once. If he'd anticipated what Kaycee and Pruitt could do, this would never have happened.

He knew it. And he had no way to argue himself out of it.

He drew in a deep breath and let it out. "If we hadn't gone down to the surface, those children would have died," Ethan said. As it came out of his mouth, he realized it sounded more like an excuse than an assertion of his moral high ground.

"That is true," Purnell said, nodding. "Honestly, it's because of this one extenuating circumstance that you have not already been charged with negligent homicide."

"Bluntly put, the negative publicity that would come from arresting the person that rescued the only survivors of the Starlight Colony is not something we're willing to bring down on CSL," the advisor said. "At least not unless Captain MacKenna reports something egregious in your actions."

"So far, what we've read in your reports is not a compelling argument in your defense, particularly in the face of the preliminary work being done by the crew of the *Magellan*,"

Maxwell added.

"I understand," he said. He felt the desire to fight drain from him.

"Do you have anything else you wish to add?" she asked.

"No, ma'am," he said quietly. He stared at the back of his hands on the table in front of him and shook his head.

"Then we will work our way through the steps of the process and consider our decision," she said. "You are not to leave the Galileo Station Complex and you are to remain available should more questions arise through our exploration and additional hearings. You are not expected to attend, nor are you required to participate, in these proceedings from here forward. I think it is reasonable to expect that it will take no more than a week to ten days for us to arrive at our conclusion."

"One question?" he asked before she moved to adjourn the hearing.

She nodded.

"I have a personal issue I'd like to address in New Hope City if I may. Billy Chandler's family lives in New Underhive, and I would like to meet with them to express my condolences, and to give them his personal possessions. I think it's important for me to help them understand what happened. It should take me a day at most."

She leaned back and the three of them huddled again.

"You can go," Purnell said. "Make sure you check in and out with station security, so we know your location, and limit your disclosure of details to known facts only. I advise you to avoid making statements to them that would lead to pointless conjecture that might harm your credibility before this tribunal. As I said, we won't have a decision until we work through the steps, and the insertion of irrelevant theories will adversely affect the outcome from your perspective. Do you understand what I am saying here Mr. Walker?"

"Absolutely," he said, biting down on his desire to protest her implication that he was prone to wild conjecture.

"Then you are free to go. We will inform you when the matter is settled."

What you mean to say, is that it's already been decided, he thought as he stood up and turned toward the door.

CHAPTER TWENTY-THREE

THE DRYDOCK WAS the only bar in New Hope City that Ethan knew, and it wasn't the kind of place he'd have wanted to find himself marooned in for the seven hours before his flight back to CS-1. Not that the Drydock was a dive, in fact far from it. The truth was, he met his first ex wife here and escaped his second one when she fell into the bottom of a bottle at a table in the back corner. The memories weren't something he felt inclined to deal with at the moment.

Fortunately, the food was good, and the booze was strong. The atmosphere reeked of high-end cargo captains and their ranking crewmembers. It was far from a seedy clientele, because running independent cargo ships was an expensive business. When the monthly cost of owning and operating your own starship was more than some people saw in an entire century of work, it weeded out all but the most successful.

There was cred in the room, and not a little of it. Even the relatively rich here were ambitious and smart. And dangerous, despite their polish.

Like most of the captains who worked the lines, Walker had leased the *Olympus Dawn* to keep his costs to a manageable level, but more than a few of the captains that sat and drank at the polished bar, were whole owners. A few of them had even cleared a second ship and operated them with contracted crews.

When he'd started out as a lease contract operator, he'd aimed to be among the first group, but now with the inquisition hanging over him, he knew he'd be lucky to reach even the second string again.

A real waitress walked up to his table and tapped her foot with a slight air of impatience as he scanned the menu display. "Pa, what's your pleasure?" she said. She had a touch of LEO bite in her voice.

He'd finished spending time with Billy's family, and he needed a drink. Badly.

"Double Starshine, if you still have it," he said, glancing up at her and trying to smile.

"You *are* going to eat with that?" she said, landing enough sarcasm in her tone to turn her question into advice.

He nodded, not feeling motivated to dilute the alcohol with food, but her point was valid. He pointed at a random line on the menu. It didn't matter what it was, it would make her happy, and he was sure it would resemble something edible.

"Good choice," she said, picking the display pad up and slipping it into a curvy place in her jumper. He shook his head and sighed as she walked away to get his drink. If he were in a better place, he'd have done more than notice.

His mind wandered back over the last few hours. When he showed up at Billy's parents' house, he realized that a situation he'd expected to be bad would be infinitely worse. Within minutes he'd run out of things to say.

"Billy was a good man. He was loyal. He died a hero."

"Oh, he had a wife and little?"

"I am sorry. I didn't know … He died saving children."

"No, I'm sorry I really can't say what happened … Just that he

was a hero."

"What should you tell his son? Uhm … that he was a hero."

He'd left a few of Billy's personal possessions with them and made arrangements to have the rest of his belongings delivered before he made his exit. It had been the longest two hours he'd ever experienced.

The waitress reappeared and set his glass on the table. Carefully.

They called the orange alcohol Starshine because moonshine didn't work as a name when you were sitting on the moon drinking it. As near as anyone would say, one of the bartenders made it in the back room using pure sucrose and residual heat from a waste thermal processor. Once it had reached sufficient intensity to be just short of spontaneous combustion, he then filtered it through habanero distillate or some other evil, flaming demon juice.

He used to appreciate the drink just because of its brutal honesty. It sent the warning that it was dangerous from the moment she set the glass on the table. It burned the eyes before it got close enough to drink, and kept burning all the way to the pit of the stomach, and then on down through the body as it descended back to the pit of hell where it belonged.

Starshine wasn't something a person could enjoy as much as simply endure. But it was excellent at providing the mind-numbing fog that he needed.

He gasped as he shot it back and pointed at the empty glass before the waitress had turned to walk away.

"You sure, pa?" she asked, raising a skeptical eyebrow.

"Yes," he mouthed. He nodded when he realized his vocal cords had gone into early retirement. Or had dissolved.

His second drink hit the table in the same delivery that brought his meal. He pushed it back far enough that his food was out of the fallout pattern, and then studied what she brought him to eat.

It was pretty in an odd sort of way, but he wasn't sure exactly what it was. It appeared that they'd replaced the cooking staff with something like a chem-head refugee from an art commune since the last time he'd eaten here.

There was an asymmetrical slab of something that looked a bit like seared meat protein. It was cut with an oddly sloped top and a waterfall of unidentifiable vegetables cascaded down the wedge into a reservoir of brown gelatinous goo. Shocking white and vivid green ribbons of a sauce-like substance crisscrossed the entire top of the sculpture, while sprigs of some unidentifiable orange leafy weed stuck out of random, sliced holes in the alien landscape.

On the whole plate, the only thing he could identify with any certainty was a yellow yeastcake, and it appeared to be a levee to keep the goo in place. He wasn't sure he could safely remove it to eat it.

Then to make the whole absurd creation worse, they served it with a single bamboo skewer and a short knife with a blunt hooked end. No fork. No spoon. Not even chopsticks.

He looked up to see if he could find the waitress to ask her for some professionally designed eating tools when an eclipse spread across his table.

"You're Ethan Walker?" the source of the shadow said. He looked up, *a long way*, before he saw the face attached to the surly voice.

"I was yesterday," he said, shaking his head. He recognized the tone of voice and the slur of a couple too many drinks.

"You used to master the *Olympus Dawn*?" the man asked.

"Still do as far as I know," Ethan said, shrugging and trying to smile.

"I hear different," the mountain of flesh said.

"Well then you hear things I haven't heard." *I am sure you hear different through your ass*, he thought trying to let his amusement show.

"CSL pulled your ticket," he said.

"Not from what I know." He glanced down at the table and wondered if a bamboo skewer would work as a deadly weapon in a pinch. *Not likely.*

"The Drydock is a private club for captains and crews," he said, raising his voice as he looked around the room to see who might agree with him.

"I know," he said. "But until I know otherwise, I'm still a captain. Why don't you just leave me to eat in peace?"

"You don't belong here," he said, his voice going up another notch in volume as he gained confidence in his position. Nobody had stepped in to defend Walker, so he was feeling sure of himself and it showed.

"Look, let me buy you a drink and you can go back to your table and leave me the frak alone. Fair enough?" Ethan said, trying to see if the guy could be calmed down with another drink. Not that he needed it.

"No. Really, you need to be leaving," he said.

"When I'm done with my food, I'll be more than willing to go," Walker said. "I think the air cyclers aren't clearing out the stink, anyway." Instantly he regretted that his first drink had given him some artificial confidence and had fueled his mouth to the point of saying something stupid. Looking straight ahead, he put his hands on the table beside his plate. He could see the man tense in his peripheral vision.

"You're right, it smells like a bloodcase in here ... and, oh look! That would be you that's causing it," the man said, idiotic sarcasm making his voice lose some of its power.

Ethan leaned back in his chair and scanned the room. The waitress was watching the situation as were several others along the bar. "Alright, I've had the day from hell and you've obviously made it your crusade to make it worse," he said. "I've asked you politely to go back to your cave and play with your own food like a good boy. So just get out of my face."

The man growled and leaned forward onto the table with both hands. "The rules are posted on the frakking door. Captains and officers only. You aren't either one. You're a fuck up that got his crew killed and you don't deserve to eat here. In fact, you don't deserve to eat anywhere this side of prison."

"Give it a rest Mackey," a woman said, walking up behind the idiot and putting a hand on his shoulder. She was tall and moved like a dancer. Or a fighter.

"Back out of this, Ammo," he said, glancing at her. "This isn't your problem. Don't buy yourself a share. Walker here is just leaving."

"He doesn't look like he's leaving," she said. "I think he was enjoying his dinner just fine up to the point where you landed your fat ass on his table. Why don't you go buy him a drink as a way of showing him it was just a misunderstanding on your part?"

"Why the hell—" His thought ended abruptly with a grunt as his eyes bulged out of their sockets in shock.

The hand resting on his shoulder tightened down as she turned him away from the table and shoved him toward the bar. It was only when Mackey tried to walk that Ethan realized that she'd pulled about a half meter of his undersuit out of the back of his pants, in the general direction of his shoulder blades.

Slapping both hands over his mouth Ethan tried to hold back a belly laugh so hard that it threatened to make his head explode instead. He wasn't the only one amused by Mackey's misfortune, the entire dining room erupted into laughter.

The woman sat down and grinned.

"Thanks," he said. "I don't think I've ever seen that particular technique used for bouncing a drunk."

"I call it wedgie-jitsu," she said, offering her hand. "Tiamorra Rayce, but my friends call me Ammo."

"I can see where you get the name," he said, "but I'm afraid that you might use that word a bit loosely."

"Which one?"

"Friends," he said. "I think Mackey called you by your nickname."

"It's all relative I guess," she said. "I brokered him a couple loads to Starlight and now he thinks he owns me."

"Hmph. Starlight," Ethan said, feeling a brick fall into the pit of his stomach.

She nodded. "I understand you rescued some kids from there."

He looked down at his plate and pushed it back. "Yah, thirteen of them." His voice felt like it was going to betray him, so he shut up and just shrugged.

"In my mind that makes you a big damned hero," she said, thumping the table with a finger tip to get his attention. When he looked back up at her she winked. Waving to the bartender, she held up two fingers and pointed at his glass.

"Drinks are on me." She smiled and pushed the plate back in front of him. "That is, as long as you're willing to tell me what really happened out there?"

CHAPTER TWENTY-FOUR

IT WAS DAY TEN and Ethan sat at a table in the back of the same dive bar he and Angel had eaten at their first night at CS-1. He felt like all he'd been doing since all this began was eating and drinking. He drank a lot more than he should, but it didn't matter, because he would not be going back into space any time soon.

He didn't know it officially yet, but he knew it in his gut. A steady stream of low-level intoxication helped to quiet the uncertainty.

"We got in about two hours ago," Rene said, appearing out of the crowd and landing unceremoniously in the chair beside him. "It took me this long to track you down."

"Yah, wasn't feeling much like company," Ethan said. "You just get back?"

"CSL ordered us to take the *Dawn* to Ceres Six for an inspection and service," he said. "They were backed up, so it took a few days extra."

"We weren't due for another year," he said.

"Marti took the opportunity to get some upgrades and spare parts for her Gendyne mech," he said.

"Seriously, they had you take the *Dawn* in for an inspection?"

Ethan asked. "If Ceres Six was backlogged, it wasn't just a matter of convenience."

Rene nodded.

"That's not a good sign," Walker said. He poured himself another shot from the bottle he had on the table. He didn't know if that was three or four, but the bottle was half empty.

"You drinking alone or is Angel around here somewhere?" he asked.

"She's out with one of the security escorts they assigned to me the first night we were here," Ethan said. "She accidentally flashed her tattys at her, and I think it was love from then on."

"So, you are drinking alone then," he said.

He nodded.

"You need reinforcements." Rene flagged down a bot and requested a glass.

"Where do things stand?" he asked as the servobot slipped the glass onto the table.

"Who the frak knows?" he said, filling Rene's glass for him. "They talked to me for about twenty minutes the first morning, and other than that, they've not told me anything even when I comm them."

"You mean you don't get to be part of the process?" Rene gulped down his drink and set the glass back on the table with a loud clack.

"Nope," Ethan said. "They told me that unless they need clarification, or something comes up new, they've already got enough facts to make a decision."

"They do?"

"So, they say," he said. "MacKenna had a report in their hands before we got back, and I guess they consider anything other than her word on the matter as suspect."

"She can't be done already?" Rene asked. He poured another

shot into his glass and stared at it for several seconds before he had worked up the courage to slam it down too. He hissed as it hit bottom. "I'm sure they'd have made an announcement about what happened to the colony if they knew anything."

"I'm sure the *Magellan* might still be investigating that, but that's not relevant to the tribunal. All they're worried about is my misconduct," he said.

"Then why does it take so long?"

"Bureaucratic crap," Walker said. "They have to hold a few meetings and a public hearing. It's probably all about covering their asses against liability. Once they polish the legal turds, then they burn me at the stake, and it's done."

"What about witnesses?" he asked. "Don't you get to argue your side?"

"What about them? Basically, they work from the idea that witnesses can only interpret facts incorrectly. They didn't say it quite that way, but that's the impression I got." He shrugged. "Facts are facts, and there's no point in trying to change them. No room for alternative facts in the real world."

"You're saying they can convict you without a chance to address the allegations?" he said. "That's totally foobed."

"There's no alleged anything," Ethan said, snorting. "I got caught doing stupid things, and I should have known better. Plus, it's not a trial, anyway. They told me upfront they won't send me to prison."

"That's a good thing, but why?"

"Because it would stink up their public relations to put a hero in jail." He laughed.

"I saw the newswave about us rescuing a bunch of kids," Rene said. "It was short on details but did make you smell good."

"Yah. I'm still trying to get that into my head somehow. I get my crew killed because I'm stupid, and then I end up a frakking hero on the 1800 newswave."

Ethan reached for the bottle, but Rene poured himself another and set it down out of reach. "You are a hero you know," he said, taking a smaller sip of the rum.

Walker shook his head. "No, I'm an idiot. They were right. I could have kept it from happening."

"No, you couldn't," he said, his face showing he wasn't buying it. "More importantly, if you hadn't gone down there, you'd never have found those kids."

"Yah. I know," he said. "But Billy and Preston would be here sharing a drink with me and not... gone."

He leaned forward and reached for the bottle again and Rene slid it further out of reach. Walker sighed but pulled his hand back. "I should have stopped Pruitt from getting the shuttle and going down there," he said. "I knew he could fool Marti, and I didn't do anything to prevent it. A good captain anticipates problems and is proactive, not reactive. That's why they're after my certs. I was too dumb to get in front of the situation."

"When do you get to hear the final results of their inquiry?" he asked.

"The public hearing was this morning," he said. "I wanted to go but they wouldn't let me."

"You couldn't even go to a public hearing on your case?" The engineer shook his head and frowned. "That's not right."

"I asked about that," Ethan said. "They told me it was so that anybody who wanted to talk wouldn't feel intimidated to speak their mind with me being there."

"So, you still haven't said when you'll know?" Rene asked again.

"Dono." Ethan shrugged. "Tomorrow maybe, unless someone said something today that opened up something new."

"Well then, maybe we should get you back to your suite," he

said. "You could use some sleep before morning."

Walker sighed and nodded, sliding his chair back with a little too much energy and almost knocking the table over behind him. "Sorry," he said as the man behind him growled.

Rene smiled and held the bottle out to the man as a peace offering. It worked, and he grinned as he took it.

"Let's go," Rene said, grabbing Ethan by the arm and steadying him as he tried to help him to his feet.

"Not yet," Nuko said. She pushed her way up to the table and shook her head. Her face looked like she had been crying. She crashed down into the chair across from Walker and tossed her thinpad on the table. "So, you've heard?"

"Heard what?" Rene said as he eased himself back into his chair.

"I just got told to post for a new position," she said. "They've sold out the lease on the *Olympus Dawn* and I've got twenty-four hours to vacate or apply to the new owner." She looked at the two glasses on the table, one empty, and one almost full. Without asking, she grabbed Rene's and swallowed it in a single gulp.

"They told you to leave the *Dawn*," Ethan said, his heart falling through his chest and out onto the table. He felt empty. Drained. "They haven't notified me yet."

"They sold it out?" Rene asked. "Not another lease-hold?"

She shook her head. "The orders say the title is in escrow and the new owner will post for positions once the transfer closes."

"I guess that tells me what the decision is." Walker picked up his empty glass and stared at the bottom. "There's no point in me going home to bed now."

Rene's comm notification chirped in his pocket. Pulling out his thinpad, he glanced at the screen and nodded. "Me too."

"Time for another bottle," Ethan said. This time Rene didn't stop him.

CHAPTER TWENTY-FIVE

ETHAN DIDN'T REMEMBER getting back to his suite, but somehow he woke up in a bed. Alone and naked, but not smelling like he'd done anything too embarrassing. That was a relief. Or a disappointment, and he wasn't sure which.

He didn't feel too bad until he tried to sit up and the room spun sidewise while his body did end-overs. It was like somebody had put his brain in a blender and then turned off the gravity.

Obviously, he wasn't alone although he was alone in the bedroom. He could hear voices coming through the wall. Muffled, but ringing his skull like a bell.

He heard Angel and maybe her girlfriend of opportunity, but there were others too. Rene? Nuko? He didn't want to talk to anyone.

Especially not them.

They'd have to be leaving to get their stuff off the ship, anyway. Unless they'd posted to the new owner and then … and then, he didn't want to think about that.

The memory flood gates opened, and he remembered sitting in the bar when Rene got his repost orders. Pieces of the evening from that moment were all he had, and they flashed back into his mind in waves of self-indulgent pity. He flopped back in the bed and pulled the pillow over his head.

Maybe if I lay here long enough, they'll just go away.

Suffering through the spins again, he closed his eyes and tried to think.

It was over. Everything was over. His whole life, and everything in it, was done.

Up until last night, he hadn't accepted that they'd take his Shipmaster license away for good. He'd held on to the hope that somehow through it all, doing the right thing would have been more important than doing things right.

But that's not how it worked. Not in the real world.

I don't even know how long they'll let me stay here, he realized. *I'm no longer an officer in CSL service so they might throw me out today. Maybe they'll let me pay a night or two out of my pocket and I can hang in here long enough to figure out what I'm going to do with my life.*

He had some cred put back, enough for a year if he lived smart, and the threshold disbursements would keep him from ever falling through the cracks, even if he wasn't smart.

He laid with his eyes closed on the edge of dozing off as images of places he could go to hide from the crash landing of his life drifted through his mind. In the last three years, he'd been to most of the colony worlds, so he knew about what places would be most likely to fit his needs. The only thing he knew for sure was if he couldn't fly, he'd want to be as far from the hub worlds as possible.

No place leaped out at him as being far enough away where he wouldn't end up being a rock farmer.

Another wave of grief washed over him as he raged against his own inner demons. By sheer force of will, he pulled his head back out of the fogbank that threatened to swallow him.

Rolling onto his side, he eased to a vertical position. This time the spins settled a little quicker than before, and he managed to get all the way to a standing position. He couldn't hear the voices in the other room, so they must be gone. He staggered over to the bedroom console and tapped the screen.

The chrono said it was 1310.

That can't be right. He found his thinpad and confirmed the time. He hadn't slept past 0600 in years. In fact, he didn't remember ever seeing the high side of morning from his bed.

Well, except when he had a warm body in bed with him.

Looking around the room for his clothes, he saw them folded on a chair beside the door. *Whoever got me into bed was neat. Probably Nuko.*

He smiled for a brief moment, but then the bricks of reality rained down on him again. She and Rene were going to have to post to other ships. They would be going their separate ways and he would be looking for work. On the ground somewhere.

I just have to get through the day, he thought. *None of it matters, at this point.*

"I don't have to figure this all out today," he said to himself.

"Good afternoon Captain Walker," the console's AI said, detecting his presence from his voice. "You have a message."

"Who's it from?" he asked, annoyed that the computer sounded so cheerful.

"Sender identity is blocked. It was received from a public data exchange," it said.

Blocked? Who blocks their ID?

Debt collectors and legal advisors, he realized. The first one he could ignore, at least until he had his feet back on the deck. The second one could be a problem.

Sitting down on the edge of the bed again, he sighed. "Play it."

"It is text only. Shall I read it to you?"

"Sure, go ahead," he said, looking over at his clothes and deciding he might want to scrub before he got dressed. A hot shower would help get his brain online too.

The console screen lit up, but the computer read the message aloud. "Priority delivery. Captain Walker, please report to 141-260 Promenade-Two, Cochrane Station-One, at 1600 hours today. End."

"That's all there is?" he asked, scratching his head while he leaned forward and read it again. "And there was no sender listed?"

"Negative," it said.

"What is at that address?"

"Transportation Division, Smythe Biomedical Technologies."

"Frak that can't be good," he groaned. "I bet CSL chucked me under the lander."

"Unable to formulate response," the AA said.

"I don't suppose there's anything regarding my inquiry?" he asked.

"Negative."

"How about from Nuko and Rene?" he asked. "They were here this morning, weren't they?"

"Yes," it said.

"Did they say where they were going?"

"Negative," it said. "The four other occupants of your suite left several minutes ago and left no message for you."

Not even a goodbye. Probably better that way.

He looked at his folded clothes. A basic duty uniform. Getting up he grabbed it off the chair and walked over to the recycler bin and dropped it down the chute.

Yah, better that way.

CHAPTER TWENTY-SIX

PROMENADE TWO WAS the upper deck of CS-1 and had huge bands of clear plasglass that arched high overhead and gave a view of the entire old Galileo station and the faint wispy band that was the opposite side of the huge ring. The view was stunning even for someone that had spent a large portion of his adult life traveling through space.

The only downside to living on the Upper Promenade in Ethan's mind was it was also where the creds lived. Huge grotesque piles of wealth lay hidden in the Earthlike parks and towers that rose up to, and even in some cases through, the crystal vault that held the world inside.

He didn't want to be here, but he knew he had to face the idea that the system wasn't through chewing on him. He had nothing left to bleed. He hoped that if he could just get past this moment and its probable outcome, he could walk away.

Maybe rock farming is a better future for me.

At least then, he might forget he once rode the stars.

Stepping off the slidewalk in front of his destination, he stared up at the building. It rose a dozen decks toward the sky above. Standing at the base of the tower, he couldn't tell for sure if it was one of the spires that penetrated through the enclosure but it seemed likely, since there were several ships docked to what looked like a private stanchion directly over his head.

Without thinking he sorted the vessels into classes, personal cruisers, private shuttles, and a few freighters. His heart almost ground to a halt when he saw a Percheron Class hauler like the *Olympus Dawn* docked close to the upper end of the piling.

Pulling his eyes down, he looked at the deck under his feet and shook his head. "That's my past," he said. "And this is my future."

Taking a deep breath, he let it out. "Let's get this over with." As he stepped toward the front of the building, a scanning beam swept over him and he paused. The door opened, and a voice came over the audio system. "Welcome to Smythe Transportation Center, Captain Walker. Please come in and someone will be right with you."

I'm not a captain anymore, he thought. *I've got to keep reminding myself of that.*

The inside of the building looked bigger than it had on the outside. He paused to process the view up through the center of the tower and it took him a second to realize that the illusion came from reflective partitions positioned so that they seemed to disappear when you looked directly at them.

A man appeared in front of one wall and he shook his head. He hadn't literally appeared, but rather had come around a corner that wasn't visible. As the man walked across the distance in his direction, Ethan realized that he was massive. Even more imposing than Pruitt, if that was possible.

He wore an expensive business suit that looked like it strained its structural integrity just to keep his physique contained. "Captain Walker?" the man said. "I'm Jefferson Cordwain. I've been asked to attend to your needs until the meeting starts."

Jefferson Cordwain. Good name for a legal advisor. I am

obviously so foobed here, he thought shaking the man's hand. "Actually, it's not captain anymore," he added.

Cordwain raised an eyebrow and shrugged. "I wasn't aware of a change in your status, but regardless, if you'll follow me please."

"Why am I here?" Ethan asked as he followed the man down a more normal looking hallway.

"I'm not authorized to discuss that," he said.

They'd stopped at a door and a biometric scanner swept the man's outstretched hand. "If you'll wait here, I'll let the boss know you're ready. There is coffee on the table for you, and if you need anything else, the AA will let me know."

"Real coffee?" he asked, forgetting for a moment that it felt like his life was about to spin out of control again. "Not pseudojo?"

"I believe she had them prepare Escobosa Bold for you, although it might be Boa Vista Black," he said. "Now if you don't mind, I'll let her know you're waiting."

A coffee urn sat on a sideboard and other than that and a table with eight chairs around it, there was nothing else in the room. Everything was white on white with a side of white. It felt a bit like he imagined a conference room in a very expensive hospital to be. Sterile and lifeless, but with an edge of luxury.

He had no idea how long he waited, but he'd just poured his second cup of coffee and returned to the table when the door opened.

Shaking his head in disbelief and anger, he stood up the instant she walked in.

Keira Caldwell.

"I don't have anything to say to you," he said, stepping back from the table. "Nothing personal but, well, yeah it's personal. Thanks for the coffee, but I'll be leaving now."

"Ethan, please. Wait," she pleaded, stepping around in front of him as he angled for the door.

He paused and cut back around the opposite direction and accelerated for the exit.

"I got your Shipmaster certification back," she said as his hand hit the door plate and it slid open. Cordwain leaned against the wall on the opposite side of the hall, surveying his fingernails. He looked up and shook his head.

Ethan skidded to a stop, grabbing the door jamb to swing back in Kaycee's direction. "You did what?"

"Ethan please, come back in and sit down. Finish your coffee and let's talk," she said, nodding at the chair at the end of the table and sliding his cup toward it. "If I haven't convinced you to hear me out by the time you've finished it, you're free to go."

He stepped back inside the room and set his feet. The door slid closed behind him. He crossed his arms and glared. "Let's start with what you just said. You got my licenses back?"

"Yes," she said, nodding as she turned and poured herself a cup.

He still hadn't moved when she turned back around. "Please sit down and I'll explain," she said. "There are a few things I haven't been entirely honest about, and when I realized how things were playing out, I had to make it right."

"Just get to the part where you explain how you got the tribunal to lift the suspension," he said, sitting down and picking up his coffee. "And you better talk fast because this is a small cup."

"I went to the public hearing and spoke on your behalf," she said. "I'm pretty persuasive when I want to be. And it helps that CSL earns a fair portion of its revenue from Smythe."

"So, you got Smythe to use their influence to swing the decision?"

"You could say that," she said, pulling a thinpad out of her pocket and tossing it onto the table in front of him.

He looked at it but didn't touch it. "What's that?"

"My ID. Look at it."

He set the cup down. *Half empty.* Dragging the thinpad in front of him, he glanced at it and shrugged.

"Read it." she said.

Smythe-Caldwell, Keira Jayne, MD. PhD. STIF.

"Smythe-Caldwell?" he asked.

She grinned. "My legal name has one of those snob hyphens in it, so I choose to forget the Smythe when I introduce myself."

He nodded, realizing he'd been right all along. They didn't breathe the same air.

"Ever hear of Charles Alexander Smythe?"

"The first Chancellor of the Coalition? He started this company, He crossed his arms, he glared didn't he?"

"Yah. His son married my mother. It just makes my life easier if I use her name most of the time," she said. "Unless of course I need to pull in a favor, and then it's all in the name."

"So, you leaned on them and got them to change direction on pulling my ticket," he said. He picked his cup up and took another big sip. "Thanks, but with a black mark like I've got, even with a license, nobody will hire me. CSL sold my ship out from under me and a corporate cargo company won't even look in my direction. I've got no ship, and no prospects."

"Yah, about that," she pulled the thinpad back across the table in her direction and thumbed the screen forward. "Turns out I own a ship and I'm looking for a captain."

"You own a ship?" he said.

"I do now." she said, nodding. "I just bought one."

"I'm not a yacht driver," he said, shaking his head and taking another sip of coffee. He glanced into the cup. One more sip and he was done.

"I know," she said." She pushed the thinpad back to him. The title and registration for a ship was on the screen.

He scanned over the documents and stopped when he got to the registration numbers, blinking several times before he shook his head. "What the frak is going on here?"

"I bought the *Olympus Dawn*."

CHAPTER TWENTY-SEVEN

ETHAN SWALLOWED the last of his coffee and pushed back from the table. Shaking his head, he frowned. "Sorry, something is twisty here."

"No, it's clean," she said. "I closed on it yesterday before your hearing."

"I'm sure you did, but I'm even more sure there is something stinking in the boiler room." He stood up.

"I wanted to make sure I saved your ship for you," she said.

Her eyes looked like she was serious, but it was too far from believable to be true. "Why did you do that?" he asked, leaning forward and picking up the thinpad again to scan it.

"Because I thought it might be a good investment?" she said, shrugging. "I don't want to own the ship itself, since I know nothing about freelance shipping. I just plan to turn the title over to the captain. Once *you* say yes."

"I appreciate what you're offering, but I know how much the *Dawn* had to cost you. You don't make that kind of 'investment' without wanting something for it. As much cred as you had to swing to do it, those are going to be some damned hefty strings."

He couldn't believe he was about to walk out on the one thing he wanted more than anything. But he was pretty sure that was exactly what he was going to do. "Thanks for the coffee and for getting my Shipmaster certs cleaned for me."

"Don't you want to know what I want in exchange for it? Before you leave?"

He hauled in a heavy breath, holding it for several seconds before he let it leak back out. He set his hands flat on the table and tensed to push himself away, but he just couldn't do it.

Frak. I have to know.

"Fine. Tell me," he said, looking down at the empty cup. "You're on borrowed time so talk quick."

"All I want is the right to pick some of the jobs you take. Only once in a while." She looked up at him, and her face said there was something else she wanted to add to that statement.

The caveat of doom.

"Pick some jobs?" he asked. "I won't carry illegal cargo, so if that's what you're thinking we're done."

"Oh no, nothing like that," she said, her face showing genuine shock at the suggestion.

"Then what kind of jobs?"

"You know I lost almost my whole family on Starlight, and I can't let that go without looking into it more thoroughly," she said. "The jobs I am talking about would be things that might shine some light into the corners of what happened."

"You need a science vessel for that," he said. "The *Olympus Dawn* is a cargo ship."

"I know that. But they've quarantined the whole system, so we couldn't get close enough to do a study, anyway." She paused and cocked her head to the side. "Have you read any of the reports from the *Magellan* yet?"

"I've tried not to. It burns a bit looking at what happened," he said. "And I didn't think they'd released anything yet."

"Not officially," she said. "Elias is still out there, and he's pushed me a little of the inside scan. They're saying it was a virus."

"That sounds plausible," Walker said. He eased himself back into his chair. He wasn't sure he would keep his seat, but her proposal intrigued him enough to listen a while longer.

"No, it doesn't," she said. "You were clean when you came back. We all were."

"Just because we didn't step in the alien goo, doesn't mean it's not possible."

"Then explain the power drain that took out Marti's automech," she challenged. "Every bit of the hardware in the entire colony was wiped clean and sucked to the bone."

"That is odd," he acknowledged.

"Unfortunately, that isn't the thing that bothers me the most." She leaned forward and set her elbows on the table. "If it was a virus, explain to me why trained medical staff would lock those kids in a room with an open air vent?"

He drummed his fingers on the arm of his chair. "And then they set up an explosive trap to protect them. You don't use a bomb to stop a virus."

"Exactly my thought," she said.

"Let's say I agree that things stink like a blown recycler line," he said. "What do you expect to do with a freighter? If they've locked down K-186, we won't be able to stick our nose in there."

"Right now, I don't have any ideas," she said. "What I do know is that indie crews talk to each other, and if something is blowing sidewise, they'd be the ones to know."

"You bought the *Olympus Dawn* so I could chase rumors for you?"

She nodded. "So, we can."

"We?"

"Yah you need a ship medic," she said. "I think I might be qualified."

And there's the caveat, he thought.

"You are frakking with me, yes?" He laughed at the absurdity of the idea. "You're the heir to one of the ten wealthiest families in the entire Coalition, and you expect me to believe you want to roster in on a freighter crew."

"Well, losing the investment we put into Starlight almost put Smythe Biomedical into receivership," she said, smiling with half her face. "It was a huge gamble, and we crapped out."

"What exactly was your wager in that blasted piece of barren dust?" he asked. "It certainly wasn't going to become a vacation destination for the rich and ludicrous."

"There were mineral deposits that are essential to recreating one of the Shan Takhu medical devices," she said. "It was how we swung the lease on the proxy chamber we were carrying."

"The what?"

"It would take a while to explain," she said. "Let's say it's one of the most important technologies to come out of the Tacra Un, and the only place we've found this critical mineral is on Shadetree."

"So your family was bankrolling a mining mission in hell." he said. "That doesn't change your royal lineage."

"Do you know how much I resent that?" she said, the flash in her eyes telling him he'd landed on a raw nerve.

"I can't believe I'm even considering this," he said, getting up and walking over to pour himself another cup of coffee.

"I can't believe I'm doing it either," she said. She grabbed the thinpad and scrolled to the end of a long file before she pressed her thumb against the screen. "That's the contract transferring title. The *Olympus Dawn* is yours."

She handed it to him. "No strings."

He stared at the file for almost a minute, unable to make his mind focus on the writing. His hands shook as he struggled to accept the reality that the ship was really his.

"Just seal the transfer," she said.

He set the thinpad down on the table and pressed his thumbprint onto the screen beside hers.

"Now, Captain Walker, since you have several positions you will need to fill, I would like to post formally as chief medical officer of the *Olympus Dawn*. I think I'm qualified," she said. "If you choose me for your crew, I assume there's some kind of standard contract I'll need to execute so you'll feel comfortable that I won't overstep."

He nodded. "If I can somehow wrap my brain around the insane reality of you wanting to serve on a freighter, I will need to set one condition right up front. While I'm willing accept the idea that you might have jobs you'd like us to take, when you're on my ship, you will never contradict an order I give. This applies whether it's for your mission or one we get through normal channels."

"Agreed," she said. "Your authority is absolute."

"Then I think we've got a deal," he said. "Now if you don't mind, I think I need to catch my old crew before they post to another ship."

"I don't think that will be a problem," she said, grinning. "They're all waiting in the hall."

"They are?"

"I knew you'd have some vacancies to fill."

THE END

Get *Wings of Earth: 2 - Dust of the Deep* now to ride along with the crew of the *Olympus Dawn*.

Thank you for reading **_Wings of Earth: 1 Echoes of Starlight_**. If you enjoyed the story, please take a moment and consider leaving a review.

http://ericmichaelcraig.com/review/

Reviews feed the creative souls of all authors and are invaluable in helping readers discover new books to experience.

Thank you. EMC

Archaeology is a dirty business.

Out in the Deep, it's dangerous too.

After almost losing his Shipmaster's licenses, Captain Ethan Walker takes on three new crewmembers and the first job that will get him back into space. Fortunately, the load pays exceptionally well. When he discovers that the supplies and personnel they're carrying aren't the type of payload the *Olympus Dawn* usually hauls, he realizes he has no other options. They must complete the run regardless of the danger.

Things get worse when Walker makes a one hundred light-year detour to pick up an archaeologist who knows their destination, only to find that someone has kidnapped her. Planetary security is looking for answers.

Answers he doesn't have.

Before they find out where they're headed Ethan learns they've attracted the attention of the renegade captain Kendrick Jetaar, and that he will stop at nothing to capture their cargo.

Captain Walker must escape the ruthless pirate lord before he and his crew become casualties in a war he didn't know existed.

http://mybook.to/WingsofEarth_2

Other works by Eric Michael Craig

Atlas and the Winds
Book One: Stormhaven Rising
Book Two: Prometheus and the Dragon
Box Set: Atlas and the Winds

Shan Takhu Legacy
Book One: Legacy of Pandora
Book Two: Fulcrum of Odysseus
Book Three: Redemption of Sisyphus
Box Set: Shan Takhu Legacy

Wings of Earth
Book One: Echoes of Starlight
Book Two: Dust of the Deep
Book Three: Chains of Dawn
Book Four: Beyond the Edge
Book Five: Stranger Bedfellows
Book Six: Ghost in the Dark
Book Seven: Hope Dies Hard
Box Set: Wings of Earth: Season One
Novella: Scatter the Winds

Short Story
Ghostmaker

ABOUT THE AUTHOR

Eric Michael Craig is a Hard Science Fiction writer living in the Manzano Mountains of New Mexico. He is the former Director

of Research for a private consulting laboratory in Phoenix, where he experimented with inertial propulsion and power generation technologies.

Fascinated with the "cacophony of humanity," he dedicated much of his life to observing society and how people relate to each other and the world around them. Ultimately this drove him to write full time.

When not writing, Eric is active in Intentional Community Design, plays guitar and bass, occasionally dabbles in art of various forms, and designs websites. He also owns way too many dogs.

Eric is a founding member of the SciFi Roundtable. The SFRT is an active online group dedicated to supporting indie and traditional authors by networking them with other writers and professional resources.

Connect with the Eric at: ericmichaelcraig.com
Facebook: facebook.com/ericmichaelcraigauthor/ and
facebook.com/groups/wingsofearthuniverse
Twitter: @EricMCraig
Amazon Author Central: http://author.to/emc
BookBub:https: bookbub.com/profile/eric-michael-craig

Sign up for Eric's newsletter to keep up on new releases and special features about his science fiction worlds and technologies.

http://ericmichaelcraig.com/subscribe

ACKNOWLEDGEMENTS

Thank you, Thomas Brass for answering a question in my newsletter. You gave me an excellent character and I hope you enjoy her journey. And thank you to my editor, Ducky Smith, without her there would be no Wings of Earth.

Made in the USA
Columbia, SC
09 November 2021

48686456R00133